FORGET THE PAST

FORGET THE PAST

•

CINDI DEGEYTER

AVALON BOOKS
THOMAS BOUREGY AND COMPANY, INC.
401 LAFAYETTE STREET
NEW YORK, NEW YORK 10003

PRINTED IN THE UNITED STATES OF AMERICA
ON ACID-FREE PAPER
BY HADDON CRAFTSMEN, SCRANTON, PENNSYLVANIA

FORGET THE PAST

Chapter One

P ain was the first sensation Tricia felt as she regained consciousness. Although she tried, Tricia could not remember where she was or what had happened. Moaning softly, she struggled to open her eyes.

Her vision seemed fuzzy, with everything oddly out of focus, but there was no mistaking it. She was in a hospital emergency room. The gleaming equipment, the antiseptic smell, the hard bed, and starched cotton sheets against her skin left no doubt as to her whereabouts.

"Hello," came a voice, distinctly masculine, yet as smooth and welcoming as any voice Tricia had ever heard. The voice seemed to be echoing from somewhere far away, yet she sensed that the person who owned it was near.

I'm dreaming, she told herself, closing her heavy eyelids, but the voice continued encouragingly.

"Don't go away again. I saw you open your eyes. I know you're awake. Can you hear me?"

Tricia started to nod her answer, but she found that the simple act of moving her head caused a new wave of intense pain and nausea to sweep through her body. She lifted her hand to her aching head, her long, slender fingers resting on her forehead.

"I know it hurts. Just lie still," came the same comforting voice. "I'm Dr. Randall Land," he said slowly, patiently, as if explaining some great mystery to a child. "You've been unconscious. Do you understand what I'm saying?"

With great effort Tricia turned her head toward him and saw indistinctly a man sitting in a chair next to her bed, leaning toward her, his forearms resting on his sturdy legs. From what she could see as her vision began to clear, he appeared to be quite attractive, with compelling brown eyes; firm, not craggy or rugged features; and a tall, athletic build.

"That's much better," he said in a positive tone. "You had us all worried. You have a concussion, and you've been sleeping for quite some time." His voice was characterized by a hint of humor, a casualness Tricia thought unusual in his profession.

Tricia continued to stare at him blankly as he straightened in his chair, picked up a folder from the bedside table, and took a ballpoint pen from his pocket. "I'm afraid I have to bother you for some information. Just a technicality," he reassured her. "And there's a form for you to sign." Tricia watched as he crossed his left leg carelessly over the right, the ankle of one foot resting on his other knee, balancing the folder on his thigh.

"My head hurts," Tricia whispered, barely audible, lifting her hand again to touch her aching head.

"I'll get you something for the pain," he said, rising. Without knowing why, Tricia found something reassuring and calming in his voice. She watched as he walked across the room and saw the door open and then shut again.

Tricia closed her eyes as a defense against the pain. She tried to remember. The early fall day had been clear and crisp, with the sun warm on her skin. As she worked amid the flowers she had planted in the spring, preparing the beds for winter, the fragrance of the jasmine, as well as the smell of the smoke of someone burning fallen leaves somewhere in the neighborhood, had filled her with a feeling of contentment. She had, indeed, found the small-town attitude and life-style that she had moved to Asheville in search of. She had made progress in her quest to build a new life, leaving her past behind. She wanted to find the roots she had never felt. She sought both independence from her past and acceptance in the present.

As Tricia thought of these things, her long blond hair had fallen into her face, and she had straightened to a sitting position from bending over the flower beds to push it out of the way.

But what had happened next? She tried to remember, but the throbbing in her head would not allow her to concentrate.

Soon Tricia heard the door open again, and she listened as the doctor's footsteps approached her bed. "Where am I?" she asked in a whisper without opening her eyes and held out an open hand to receive the medication he had gone after.

"You're at Asheville Community Hospital," he said in a friendly tone, "and I've brought an injection, not a pill. So if you'll roll over onto your side. ... "

Too weak to launch an effective protest, she reluctantly rolled slowly to her side, then held her breath and squeezed her hands into tight fists as she felt him skillfully give the injection and pull the covers back over her. "Now, that wasn't so bad, was it?" he asked rhetorically.

Randall sat in his chair again. "Back to your chart. There is some information we need, then we can move you into a private room."

A private room, Tricia thought in dismay. "I want to go home," she whimpered, feeling unwanted tears well involuntarily in her eyes.

"You will, Ms. McGill. You can go home, probably tomorrow. But you have an injury, possibly severe, and we'll need to watch you closely for a few hours."

"What happened to me?" she asked, feeling helpless and confused, hating those feelings but unable to rise above them.

"It seems your head stopped my nephew's first home run hit," he answered in a voice tinged with amusement.

"A baseball?" she asked, as if what he told her was impossible. "I was hit by a baseball? I don't even like sports."

"You were outside working in your garden. My sister, Emily, lives next door. Her boys and I were playing baseball with a few friends and Matthew hit the ball much harder than any of us thought he could."

Randall paused, but when Tricia offered no comment, he continued. "Emily helped me with most of the paperwork. I have your name, address, and so on, but now I need to know some things about you." He paused briefly, glancing at the chart he held, then continued. "Are you married? Or divorced or separated?"

"No," she whispered. "No, not married."

He made a notation. "I need the name of your closest relative not living with you."

"I live alone," she answered, the fog of confusion and pain keeping her from comprehending the question he was asking.

"So Emily tells me. What about your parents?"

"Just an aunt and uncle. In Houston." Tricia told Randall the name and phone number of her aunt and uncle, the people who had adopted her when she was five years old. That was nearly seventeen years ago. She had never known her father and could not remember much about her mother. But she could clearly remember her mother's face. Its beauty had haunted Tricia from her earliest memories. With an unsettled mind, Tricia remembered her mother's light, shining hair and youthful, smiling face.

Attracted by her mother's beauty, many strange men had passed through the shabby apartment where they had lived. Tricia had been frightened by these men. She would stay in her room, cradling a favorite toy until her mother came for her. Usually the men did not even know she was in the apartment.

One night Tricia had heard her mother's muffled scream. Strange choking noises made their way into Tricia's room through the thin walls of the apartment. Terrified, she listened to the heavy footsteps of a man hurriedly leaving her mother's room, then heard the door to the outside hallway open and slam shut. She waited for her mother to come in and tell her that everything was all right, but she had never come. Tricia had hidden under the bed that night, whimpering, crying softly, cuddling her doll. She waited all night, but "Mommy" still didn't come.

Finally, as the morning light slowly chased the darkness and cold from her room, Tricia—desperately frightened and hungry—had somehow found the courage to open her door and walk slowly to the next room, where her mother lay motionless on the bed, her blue eyes open but not seeing.

After trying desperately to awaken her mother's lifeless form, Tricia had gone to the telephone and dialed "O" for the operator, as her mother had taught her. Summoned by the operator who had listened to the panic-stricken child's story, the police had come, and the trembling little girl with the tear-streaked face had led them to her mother's body. Later in the day her aunt and uncle, shaking their heads sadly, had packed her few belongings and taken her to Houston to live with them.

Jim and Barbara McGill weren't prepared for a child. They had never planned to have children, but they had, from that day, done the best they could for her, despite the fact that they often felt overwhelmed by their sudden parenthood and by the noticeably beautiful but frightened, withdrawn child. As Tricia grew older, they had talked about the horrible event. Still, Tricia grew to think that she had overheard her mother's murder and the killer's escape.

"Ms. McGill?" came the gentle voice from her bed-side, calling Tricia back into the present. "Are you still with me?"

"Yes," she answered as she felt the doctor take her hand and feel her wrist for a pulse. She felt strength in his fingers, the same strength she had seen in his eyes, heard in his voice. *I wish he'd hold my hand forever,* she thought dreamily. *It's been so long since anyone held my hand, I'd forgotten how good it feels.*

"Open your eyes, please. I need to look at them. Then the nurses will move you into a private room." He released her hand. "Also, Emily has taken the liberty of going into your house and getting a few personal items for you. She thought you might prefer your own night-clothes to that hospital gown you're wearing now. I hope you don't mind. She meant well."

"Thank you," Tricia whispered.

"Also, she asked me to assure you that she had locked your house, so you wouldn't worry."

"She's very thoughtful."

"Oh, yes, thoughtful and helpful. Almost to the point of being nosy and meddlesome." He laughed softly, probably at some family joke she couldn't understand, but she was grateful to Emily for her kindness. "The nurses will help you get settled into your room and change if you feel up to it. I'll be back to check on you in a few hours."

"Thank you, Doctor . . . Doctor. . . . " With embar-rassment, Tricia realized that she had forgotten his name.

"Call me Randall. What shall I call you?"

"Patty Ann," she murmured without thinking.

"Patty Ann?" he asked in puzzlement, shaking his

head and making a notation on her chart. "I thought your name was Tricia."

"Oh, yes," she said with an unmistakable note of sadness in her voice. "I forgot." The two large tears reappeared in her blue eyes and began a path down her face, leaving wet traces on her flawless complexion. "My name is Tricia."

"It's going to be okay, Tricia," he said, patting her hand in a brotherly manner, but his tone betrayed his confident words. "You just get some rest."

"Keep close watch on Ms. McGill," Randall whispered to the nurses. "And call me immediately if there are any changes."

Tricia felt herself being wheeled out of the room, out of his presence.

In the morning Tricia awoke feeling somewhat better than the day before. She changed into a pretty, feminine nightgown of light pink with rows of lace-edged ruffles around the neck and full sleeves. Then, taking great care to avoid the painful knot on the back of her head, she slowly brushed her long hair, which floated like a golden mist past her shoulders and behind her on the pillows. Tricia tired before she could apply her makeup, and when breakfast was brought in, she found she had no appetite.

With the bed adjusted so she was nearly sitting, Tricia lay back against the pillows, closed her eyes, and drifted into a light sleep.

The feeling of a weight settling on the edge of the bed caused Tricia to open her eyes again, and there sat the doctor from yesterday, taller, younger, and more handsome than she had remembered, and smiling mysteriously.

"Good morning, Ms. McGill," he said softly. "Feeling better, I hope."

"Yes," she answered, feeling suddenly self-conscious. "Much better, thank you. And thank you for taking care of me yesterday. I'm lucky you were at Emily's house when the accident happened." She spoke carefully, trying not to move her head.

"So you remember. That's good."

"I remember you told me that you're Emily's brother. You're the one she talks about all the time, no doubt." Her voice was soft and lyrical, capable of lulling the listener into a dream state, like the sirens who called to Odysseus as he sailed to Greece. "You said I had been hit on the head by a baseball and that I had a concussion."

"Yes, Emily is quite frantic, because it was Matthew who hit the infamous ball. She's definitely the motherly type, and I'm afraid you're about to be adopted. She's at home cooking for you now. After I bring you to your house, she'll be over to look after you."

"There's really no need," Tricia protested weakly.

"She enjoys it. Besides, you really are going to need some help for a while. That was quite a hit you took. We'll have to limit your activities, not that you'll feel like doing much anyway."

Tricia looked at him, not knowing what to say as he took her hand.

"Now," he said, looking directly into her eyes, the characteristic casualness she had noted before gone from his voice, "what is your name?"

"Tricia," she answered, "Tricia McGill."

Randall smiled with obvious relief. "Yesterday you told me it was Patty Ann. I was afraid your injury might have been more severe than I had originally thought. I came here during the night to look over your X rays again. I couldn't figure it out. A blow to the head can cause amnesia in some rare cases, but I've never known of anyone who forgot their name and took on a different one."

"Patty Ann was a childhood name," she explained. "My complete name is Patricia Ann McGill. Tricia and Patty Ann are both nicknames. You needn't have worried."

"I should have realized that," he said. "I feel amazingly stupid. Patricia Ann, Tricia, Patty Ann. Reminds me of the old nursery rhyme, 'Elizabeth, Lizzy, Betsy, and Beth, all went together to find a bird's nest. They found a bird's nest with five eggs in, they each took one and four left in.' They were all the same person, all nicknames for Elizabeth."

"I like your poem. Did you make it up?"

"No. It's Mother Goose. Didn't anyone ever read nursery rhymes to you when you were young?"

"Another gap in my education, I suppose." Tricia smiled wearily, ignoring the reference to her childhood. "I appreciate that you worried on my account. Are all the doctors in this town as thoughtful as you are?"

"There aren't many doctors in this town," he explained, modestly ignoring her compliment. "We're close to Houston, so, understandably, most doctors prefer to practice there—excellent medical facilities, a growing population. It's an economic consideration, I'm sure. The nationwide trend is moving away from family doctors practicing general medicine in small towns.''

''I see.'' Tricia smiled despite the ache in her head. ''Well, you must have made an A plus in bedside manner. You were so kind to me yesterday.'' She studied his face—attractive, with firm features and an openness that invited confidence. Then with slight embarrassment she continued. ''I even dreamed about you last night. That you were here in this room, standing beside the bed reading my chart.''

''I was here,'' he smiled apologetically, ''but I didn't mean to disturb your rest. I peeked in on you when I came to check your X rays.''

Their eyes met, causing a moment of awkward silence, then Randall said, ''I'll need to give you a quick physical exam to make sure everything is as it should be. Then we'll talk about letting you go home.'' Tricia tensed as he picked up her hand and felt for her pulse. At his touch, a strange warmth spread through her, giving color to her face. She wondered idly if this too was a side effect of the concussion.

''You haven't eaten any breakfast, Tricia,'' he remarked, observing her untouched tray. ''You need to eat to keep up your strength. You're too thin.''

''I am not,'' she began defensively, then realizing that he meant no criticism, she abruptly stopped. ''I'll eat some lunch,'' she promised softly by way of an apology. Tricia idly wondered what he would have thought if he had seen her last Christmas, at the height of her modeling career. Steven had always said she was too thin as well. He had teased her that he'd fatten her up after they were married. But the administrators at the modeling agency insisted that she stay at one hundred pounds, not an ounce over. Since she had left modeling and moved to Asheville five months ago, she had gained steadily and now weighed one hundred and ten. She was the heaviest she'd been all her life, but she was still thin by anyone's standards, especially considering her height.

Randall was a doctor—just like Steven—but much younger and more attractive. Tricia cautioned herself against these thoughts, these feelings. Experience had taught her that physical appearances were meaningless, deceptive, and sometimes dangerous.

"Your eyes are remarkably blue," he said as he reached for a small flashlight to test her pupils. "I'm not sure I've ever seen that particular shade."

"My mother had blue eyes," she answered softly, re-membering, haunted by the wasted beauty and by all the unanswered questions the memory seemed to evoke.

"Hmm, 'had blue eyes.' Is she dead?" he asked with professional interest.

"Yes. She died when I was a child."

"A disease?"

"No, she died in an accident," Tricia lied. The lie came easily. She had told this lie, hid the truth about her mother from people for as long as she could remember, as if telling the lie often enough would change the truth. But lying always made her feel guilty somehow, as if she were responsible for the truth.

"And your father?"

"I don't know," she said simply. "My mother never married." Tricia could have lied about him too, as she always had in the past, but this time she didn't. She was suddenly weary of the pretense.

"So you were brought up by your aunt and uncle," he surmised. "I called them last night to inform them about your injury. They wanted to drive in right away, but I told them you would be well cared for. Emily told me that she had met them once, and that they were older than what she had expected your parents to be."

"Aunt Barbara was my mother's only sister, though she was much older," Tricia explained. "She and Uncle Jim had no children, so when Mother died they took me in."

"I understand," he said softly, giving Tricia the impression that, somehow, he did understand much more than their brief exchange would have allowed.

The feeling of being understood, of oneness, hung in the air until Randall spoke again, changing the direction in which their conversation had been flowing.

"Anything else I should know to add to your permanent chart?" he asked.

Tricia smiled shyly, then looked down as if to examine her perfectly manicured nails. "Put that I'm terrified of needles. Almost phobic. It's all I can do not to run screaming like a little kid." She shrugged her shoulders. "Something left over from my childhood, I suppose. If it should ever come up again, please give me a pill rather than an injection whenever possible."

Randall nodded and made a notation on her chart. "That's not really so unusual. You'd be surprised how many people feel the same way." He lifted Tricia's chin so that she looked at him. "It's nothing to feel embarrassed about."

Tricia looked up at him, grateful he hadn't laughed at her.

"You've acquired quite a reputation as a mystery person in this town, you know," he said. "No one seems to know much about you, and that's unusual in a town of this size, where everyone knows, or thinks they know, everyone else's business."

"Nothing to know," she answered with deliberate casualness. "There's nothing to know about me that's worth arousing anyone's interest."

"Somehow I don't believe that," he said, his eyes scrutinizing her. "But it's your business. I respect your right to privacy. Still, if you moved here because there's some trouble you're hiding from, and you need help, you'll find I'm a great listener."

Tricia smiled at the sincerity of his offer and relaxed visibly. *This man is remarkable,* she thought, *or extremely naive. He doesn't even know me, and yet he helped me yesterday and is offering to help me now, without even knowing what kind of trouble I might have been involved in.* Rather than comment about such things, Tricia asked, "May I go home now?"

"If you promise to eat three meals a day, take the medicines I'm going to prescribe for you, and come to my office in three days for a follow-up."

"I promise," she agreed, weary from the effort of the conversation.

"Good. I'll finish my rounds, then I'll drive you home. Emily will stop by and help settle you in."

Tricia watched Randall as he rose and walked toward the door, turning to take a last lingering look at her before stepping out into the hallway.

How nice to have someone take care of me, she thought vaguely, *how comfortable.* Then with a feeling of puzzlement she realized this was the very opposite of what she had been struggling for. She had moved here to establish her independence, to nurture self-reliance, to begin anew. It had been a deliberate choice. She could have stayed in Houston among her friends, kept her modeling job there. But she had come here, bought the old house—the Lindow place, as the townspeople had referred to it—and had it redecorated exactly to her taste. She had planted flowers in the yard. She had made a new life for herself, a life as different from the old one as possible, and she liked it. She was her own person, in control of her own life, responsible only for herself and to herself, until. . . .

"It's that bump on my head," she muttered to herself. "In a few days everything will fall back into place."

Chapter Two

Randall drove slowly down the tree-lined streets toward Tricia's house. He noted that the leaves had almost completed their annual color change, signaling the coming of winter. Winters in southeast Texas weren't especially cold, but they could be dreary. The barren trees and the heavy, lead-colored clouds that produced not snow but rain made winter Randall's least favorite season.

Tricia's house, like Emily's, faced the park where Randall jogged each morning. The neighborhood was in a part of town that spoke to others of both money and a relaxed life-style. The houses were mostly large, older homes that had been carefully and extensively renovated so that the exteriors reflected a more graceful architectural period of the South. The yards were large and well tended, and the huge oak trees, heavily hung with Spanish moss like an old man's gray beard, made these homes highly valuable and enviable pieces of real estate.

Tricia's home had been considerably renovated since she purchased it. She had moved in when the work was nearly complete, five months ago. It now stood as a Victorian showplace, much like the exquisite gingerbread cottages that bakers prided themselves on making at Christmastime.

As he turned the car into her driveway, Randall realized just how much the appearance of Tricia's house mirrored the appearance of Tricia herself, a look of delicate beauty, almost too perfect to be real.

The yard dazzled with color from the many flowers she had planted and tended. Dominating the scene were yellow autumn chrysanthemums, which blazed with the brilliance of the sun.

Randall stopped the car, stepped out, and walked briskly to the passenger side to help Tricia from the car. As they walked toward the front door, Randall reached into his pocket and withdrew the keys to Tricia's house. "Emily gave me these, in the event we arrived before she had lunch ready," he explained.

"Oh," Tricia said uncertainly as he opened the door and she stepped inside. "I thought Emily would already be here."

Randall stepped in behind her and set Tricia's keys on a small table in the entryway. "Does it make you uncomfortable that she isn't?" he asked, remembering her earlier nervousness. Could a woman this beautiful be timid around men? he wondered. "I can call Emily if this is a problem for you."

"No," Tricia said so softly that Randall turned to her, slightly alarmed at the absence of vitality in her voice.

"Are you okay?" he asked. "Maybe I should have kept you under observation a while longer." He put his arm around Tricia's tiny waist protectively and led her toward the sofa. "Will this be comfortable, or shall I take you upstairs?"

At Randall's last question Tricia suddenly understood why she had reacted to him the way she had. The realization made her legs unsteady, so she had no choice but to collapse onto the sofa he had led her toward. The bump on her head had nothing to do with the strange feelings she sensed when Randall put his arms around her. It didn't explain the way her heart suddenly stopped beating momentarily and her face had paled, then colored, when he had asked if she wanted him to take her upstairs. She, Patricia Ann McGill, who had scoffed at teenage crushes and declarations of love at first sight, was undeniably drawn to Randall Land in a way she hadn't believed existed, except in fiction.

"Tricia?" he asked with concern, and he reached out, his strength supporting her small frame, gently leaning her back onto the pillows of the sofa. "Tricia?"

"I'm fine," she managed to say, forcing a calm tone despite her inward quaking and the dull throbbing beginning in her head. *This can't be happening!* she scolded herself.

Randall sat beside her and regarded her intently with assessing eyes, then he glanced around the room. "You've done a wonderful job on this house," he remarked, observing the hundreds of small decorator touches that blended together perfectly in the soft peach and mint living area, accented with live green plants in gleaming brass pots. "No one would recognize the old Lindow place."

"Thank you." Tricia smiled, grateful for the safe harbor of a conversation revolving around something other than herself. "Do you know Mr. Lindow?"

"Yes. He was a friend of my father's. He's one of my patients now. Quite a character, Harry Lindow, always doing something unexpected. His age has been catching up with him lately, but in his day he was quite a practical joker."

"Yes. I got that impression the few times I've spoken with him. And I also think he loved this house. It's a shame he reached the point where he was unable to keep up the house and had to sell it."

"I've often wondered if his son was too quick to convince him that he should sell the house and move into the nursing home. After his heart attack he was very ill and the house fell into disrepair, but Harry has improved steadily. There's really no need for him to be dependent on others now. He'd probably be much happier in a home of his own, or with his family."

"You mean his children . . . ?"

"He only has one son, and he lives out of state now. I guess John just didn't want to bother with taking care of Harry." Randall shook his head sadly. "There were hard feelings between them at one time, and perhaps the old wounds haven't healed completely. Or maybe Harry insisted on staying in this town with his friends."

"He seems like such a dear old man. It's hard to believe he's alienated from his family. And the thought of him losing his home is so sad. I almost feel guilty about buying it.''

"But you must love it, don't you, especially since all the remodeling is complete?"

"The house turned out lovely," Tricia said, her eyes traveling the room as if observing it from the viewpoint of a stranger. "But that's not what initially attracted me to it. Not really. It's the setting. The town, and especially the location of the house. The way it overlooks the park gives it such a feeling of spaciousness. I felt so confined in the city, as if I were suffocating."

"Do your aunt and uncle live in an apartment?"

"No. I did. I lived in an apartment for almost three years, but it was only the last few months that really disturbed me. So I left the noise and the crowds behind and bought this place."

"You lived in an apartment for three years? Alone?" he asked in puzzlement. "But you're only—"

"Twenty-one, almost twenty-two. I haven't lived with my aunt and uncle since I was eighteen," she answered.

"You left home at eighteen?" He seemed surprised. "That's very young. Was there trouble at home?"

"No." Tricia smiled slightly with a faraway look in her eyes, the same haunting smile Randall had been intrigued by that morning in the hospital. "No hard feelings."

Sensing that she didn't want to discuss the reason why she moved out on her own at an early age, Randall changed the topic of conversation. "Do you like it here? It's not always easy for big-city people to adapt to small-town life. Have you enjoyed your home the way you thought you would?"

"Oh, yes," she said softly. "It's exactly what I came looking for. I suspect I was always a small-town girl at heart."

"And so you no longer feel as if you're suffocating?"

"I have space here, and I enjoy the work in my flower beds."

"Yes. I've seen you working in your yard."

She looked at him quizzically.

"I jog in the park every morning," he explained. "And I've noticed you."

Tricia blushed, the rose color highlighting her pale complexion.

Randall turned away politely when he saw her discomfort at his confession. An atrium-style patio filled with blooming plants caught his attention. "Are those daffodils?" he asked, amazed to see the springtime plants thriving.

"Some people call them daffodils. They're narcissus. The flower is named for the character Narcissus in Greek mythology." She paused for a moment and then continued. "Narcissus was a beautiful young Greek man who fell in love with his own appearance. He would spend hours lying beside a pond, looking at his reflection, admiring himself. A Grecian nymph, Echo, fell in love with him, but he rejected her. His self-love overshadowed any feelings he may have felt for her. The gods were angered by his conceit, and so they turned him into a flower right there beside the pond so he could gaze at his reflection for eternity."

"Poetic justice," Randall returned. "You like that story?"

"It teaches a lesson." She looked at Randall, her clear

blue eyes seeming to beg understanding. "Beauty isn't always a gift. It can also be a curse."

"And so you keep the flowers to remind yourself of that lesson?" he asked perceptively.

She looked into his eyes without answering as the doorbell sounded. Emily had arrived.

"Come on in," Bradley said, opening the door of his home to Randall. Emily's husband was a large, tall, good-natured man who had played high school and college football, then settled down to a small-town life of selling real estate, bringing up children, and adding a few pounds each year to his once-lean frame. His life agreed with him, and he always seemed in amiable spirits. "Get comfortable. Emily will be over there pestering that poor woman for a while, I suppose," he said good-naturedly. "She just loves it when there's someone to fuss over. Maybe she should have been a doctor like you, huh?"

"I don't think a little fussing will hurt Tricia," Randall offered, moving a newspaper and several toys to make room for himself on a chair in Emily and Bradley's family room. "She tries to act self-sufficient and aloof, but I'm not so sure about her. She's very young"—he paused to puzzle over a thought—"and whatever it is she's hiding, she's careful to not give out any information."

"You mean you didn't find out anything about her while she was in the hospital?" Bradley asked curiously, seating himself in a chair opposite Randall.

"Not much. Just that she was reared by an aunt and uncle, an older couple, and that her mother died when she was young."

"I don't want to sound like one of those gossipy old women, but with her living right next door, the question has entered my mind as to why she lives alone and how she gets her money. She doesn't seem to have a regular job."

"I guess quite a few people have wondered that, and I must admit I was a little more than skeptical myself. It's quite a puzzle, leaving the excitement of the city and moving here, especially a woman as beautiful as Tricia."

"So you noticed, huh?" Bradley interrupted in a tone of amusement. "Somehow I had the feeling you didn't like her without even having met her."

Randall shrugged. "Maybe I blamed her for buying Harry Lindow's house, for leaving him with nowhere to go. Perhaps because of my affection for Harry, I lost sight of the fact that it was Harry and his feelings toward John that caused his isolation. I unjustly laid the blame on Tricia."

"And now? What changed your mind?"

Randall considered for a moment before answering. "Yesterday, when she was hit by the ball, my initial reaction was, 'Well, now the rich snob will be angry with Matthew. She'll probably make a scene!' But I had misjudged how hard he'd hit the ball. I saw her slump forward and fall. When I reached her, she was lying on the grass, and to my surprise, she looked so vulnerable, not at all what I'd expected. Much younger. I'd never really noticed her before, not really. In my mind she was just the person who'd displaced Harry Lindow."

"Tricia didn't know it was Harry's house. She bought an empty house, badly in need of repairs. It wasn't anything personal against Harry," Bradley explained.

"She's not what I thought. Not at all," Randall reflected. "When I picked her up and carried her to my car to bring her to the hospital, I was startled. She's so light, so fragile."

"So beautiful," Bradley added for him. "Though you'd think she was trying to hide it, the way she dresses. With some makeup and the right clothes, she could be a real knockout, the kind of woman you notice in a crowd. But from what I can tell, it almost seems as if she's trying to hide her beauty, to just blend in and not be noticed."

"She's come close to succeeding. But once I was near her, I found it impossible not to notice. I've never seen anything like her. It's not only her looks. She's poised and gracious, definitely not your average girl next door. I have to admit that she is without a doubt the most remarkably exquisite woman I've ever seen."

Bradley, unlike his wife, had no inclination to play matchmaker for Randall. He allowed Randall's confession to pass without comment. "So what's she doing in this little town, keeping to herself all the time?" he questioned.

"I honestly can't figure that one out."

"She paid cash for the house," Bradley mused aloud. "The way I have it figured, she's the mistress of some wealthy man who wanted her out of the city, away from his wife. Maybe it's someone well-known, so he set her up in that house: convenient, comfortable, yet inconspicuous."

"I don't think so, Bradley," Randall said, objecting to his brother-in-law's theory. "She doesn't seem the type." Randall paused thoughtfully. "Have you seen any men coming or going from her house?" he asked.

"No," Bradley answered, agreeing that his theory lacked proof. "Maybe she married some rich old man, then got his money in a divorce settlement. It's been done before—a beautiful young woman and a rich old fool."

"She said she'd never been married," Randall said, shaking his head.

"It seems unlikely, but maybe she gets her money illegally, like selling drugs," Bradley suggested as a third theory.

"She doesn't even use drugs."

"How can you be sure?" he asked, interested.

"Blood test. At the hospital we had to do blood work to check on some things, especially because she was unconscious and couldn't answer any questions. I can tell you without reservation that she doesn't use drugs."

"That doesn't give us much to go on," Bradley mused, seeming to enjoy the role of amateur detective. "Her personality puzzles me also. She never talks about herself. Also, you'd expect someone with her money and her looks to be a snob, or to use them to manipulate people. She is excessively private, but she's not snobby or manipulative, far from it. She and Emily visit, and she's great with the boys. She plays with them and sometimes she goes into Houston and comes back with toys for them, things they've wanted but we couldn't find her in town. She'll say she 'ran into it,' but some of those popular toys are hard to find. She had to have made a dozen stops to get them. She seems to genuinely enjoy the boys. And they are crazy about her. Matthew feels just terrible about the baseball thing. He thought he had killed her.''

''She'll be fine after a few days' rest and Emily's cooking, of course.'' He smiled at Bradley, that easy, relaxed kind of smile that comes from being comfortable with people and surroundings.

''Uncle Randall,'' came the joyous cry from the stairway as the four boys came tumbling down. ''Uncle Randall! Is Tricia alive? Did you bring her home?''

''Hi, boys,'' he said as they piled on him. ''Yes, she's alive, and yes, I brought her home.''

''Good. We have some presents for her,'' explained Matthew, at age seven the oldest of Emily and Bradley's four boys.

''Doctor's orders—you have to wait a day or two before you visit. She won't feel up to wrestling with you four right away.''

''You stayin' for lunch, Uncle Randall?'' Mark asked.

''Sure, if it's okay with your mom.''

''Good,'' the boys squealed in excitement.

Randall appraised them curiously. ''Why?''

''Because,'' Micah yelled, unable to contain himself, ''at dinner Momma is gonna talk you into marrying Tricia.''

''Then you can live next door,'' Matthew added, ''and Tricia will be our aunt.''

Randall looked from innocent face to innocent face. Even Marty, who was too young to add to the conversation, sensed the excitement and bounced on his chubby legs and smiled.

Bradley cleared his throat. ''Boys, why don't you get

your ball and go out in the yard?'' he said, rising and encouraging them on their way.

"But we wanna play with Uncle Randall. We wanna talk to him,'' they protested.

"You've said enough already,'' Bradley answered, corralling them to the backyard.

"You know Emily,'' Bradley said to Randall by way of an apology when he returned.

"She's been trying to play matchmaker for me for years.''

"Yes, but be careful. This time there's a real determination in her voice when she talks about you and Tricia.''

"But I'm not interested in getting married, despite her interest in getting me married. My practice takes too much of my time. It wouldn't be fair. I don't have the time nor the inclination to be a good husband. Besides, whatever the reason why Tricia came to this town, I don't think it was for husband hunting.''

Next door, Emily bustled about Tricia like an amateur nurse, settling her with pillows, covers, and a lunch tray loaded with steaming, home-cooked foods.

Then she sat down to watch over Tricia as she ate.

"Thank you, Emily,'' Tricia said as Emily took the dishes away. "But there's no need for you to fret over me. I can take care of myself.''

"Nonsense,'' Emily answered cheerfully. "That's what neighbors are for. Besides, I feel rather responsible. I should have realized that Matthew was growing stronger and getting better at sports.''

"It was an accident. I hope you weren't angry with him. Randall says I'll be just fine."

"Oh?" Emily interrupted with ill-disguised curiosity, seizing the opportunity she had been eagerly awaiting. "You finally met my brother Randall."

"Yes," Tricia answered innocently, unaware of Emily's motives.

"He's a good doctor, isn't he?"

"He was very kind to me," Tricia answered with simple honesty.

"And he is nice looking," Emily added.

"Yes," Tricia agreed wearily. "He is." Her head began to throb, and despite her gratitude for Emily's kindnesses, Tricia wished she were alone so she could rest and sort through the new thoughts and feelings that had come to her. "Where did Randall put the medicines we brought home from the hospital?"

"In the kitchen. I'll get them for you. Do you want to rest?"

"Yes," Tricia answered apologetically. "I appreciate everything you've done, but right now I feel as if I'd like to sleep."

"I understand. We can talk about Randall later," Emily said, obviously disappointed that she hadn't been able to inspire amorous feelings between Tricia and her brother.

A short time later as Tricia drifted off to sleep beneath the thick, soft comforter, Randall's face appeared to her and startled her awake. *What is happening to me?* she asked herself in dismay.

By the next day, Monday, Tricia did indeed feel much better. Her head no longer throbbed constantly, and the feeling of being confused had dissipated, leaving her mind clear once again.

"When Emily comes over today, I'll make lunch for her," Tricia told herself, feeling sure the social graces of a small town would require this. Tricia regretted her brusque dismissal of Emily the day before, when she had brought up the subject of Randall. Today she'd listen as long as Emily wanted to talk. Yesterday she hadn't felt well, but today she must begin to repay Emily's friendliness. She had moved to this town determined to fit in, to find the life-style portrayed in Norman Rockwell's paintings, the freckled-faced children waiting for the school bus on crisp autumn mornings, the women gossiping over the fence, the family picnics. If she wanted to get to know this town, Emily would be an excellent source of information. And if Emily wanted to discuss her brother, well, there were worse things! Tricia picked up the phone to call Emily.

During lunch Tricia and Emily discussed houses, Emily's children, and the neighbors, an older couple with the unforgivable vice of mowing their lawn at six o'clock each Saturday morning. Finally, Emily brought up the subject of Randall.

"Randall asked me to let him know how you're feeling. He offered to come over after he closed the office this afternoon if you needed him."

"I'm fine," Tricia assured her. "Randall's done so much for me already. He's a remarkable person. No other doctor I know would drive a patient home from the hospital.''

"Well, you have no relatives in town, Randall said it wouldn't be safe for you to drive for a few days, and there are no cabs. Besides,'' she said in a self-righteous, I'm-only-doing-it-for-your-own-good tone, "Bradley and I think it might be nice if the two of you got to know each other. You seem so right for each other.''

"Oh, Emily,'' Tricia said hesitantly. "I'm not sure that would be wise.''

"Nonsense,'' Emily objected quickly. "You've holed up in this house for five months. That's long enough. It's time you get out, have some fun! It's time for a change— something to put some color in your pale face.''

"Surely Randall already has''—Tricia groped for the appropriate words—"someone who interests him.''

Emily settled herself, as if to tell a long tale. "He did once, when he was in medical school.''

"What happened?'' Tricia asked, surprised at the intensity of her own eager curiosity.

"He and Corrie were quite in love, I believe. They certainly seemed to be. Anyway, they dated for a while. Randall planned to marry Corrie after he graduated from medical school. At first everything went well. But as time wore on Corrie grew bored. Randall had to study every evening, and Corrie wanted to go out and have fun after work.''

Tricia looked at Emily, silently encouraging her to continue.

"For a while there was just an undercurrent of disagreement. We thought they'd work it out. Later Corrie started going out alone. Eventually she met someone else.''

''And she left Randall?'' Tricia asked, unbelieving.

''Yes. He never heard from her again.''

''How sad. Was Randall devastated?'' Tricia was surprised to find that it really did matter to her that some woman she had never met could have been so callous with Randall's feelings.

''I'm sure he was very hurt. He covered it by becoming totally involved with medicine, becoming the best doctor he could be. He stayed so busy with books and patients that there wasn't time in his life for grief over Corrie.''

''What was she like?'' Tricia asked.

''Corrie? Corrie was cute. That's the only word for it—cute. Not so very pretty, but perky and round-faced. She smiled and putted equally well, and as for natural flirtatiousness, she was a master. She reminded me of the epitome of what a high school girl strives to be: bubbly and dimple-faced. Cute.''

''Didn't you like her?''

''Not really. As for myself, I've always found it hard to feel close to an adult who is cute. I can't help but wonder what becomes of them later in life, when they're too old to be cute anymore. But she did make Randall happy for a while.''

''Isn't he happy now?''

''He's not unhappy. His work suits him, and he's suited to it.''

''Then what's the problem?''

''I worry that someday he'll wake up an old man,

alone, with nothing but his work, and realize too late that work isn't enough.''

"He has friends, doesn't he?''

"Oh, yes, many friends, here and also in Houston. But Randall's not interested in parties or a full social life. He keeps himself busy with his work.''

"No girlfriends?''

"None that I know of, though many women I know wouldn't mind being considered as such. Randall is not only attractive physically, but he has one of those rare easygoing dispositions. He doesn't take himself, or his own problems, seriously. He's dedicated himself to his patients and his practice, as if there were nothing else in life. He's become a solitary man.''

Emily's voice continued, lulling Tricia into a daydream. What was it about Randall that had affected her? she wondered.

Chapter Three

On Friday morning Tricia found herself seated on an examining table in the office of Dr. Randall Land. As she waited for him to enter, she wondered if her reaction to him would be the same as it had been on Sunday, or if, because of her injury, she had reached out to him as a port in a storm. She'd spent the last half year trying to establish a sense of normalcy, of balance, in her life. She didn't need a full-blown, long-overdue case of puppy love complicating things now, when she was so close to her goal. In the five days that had passed since he had brought her home from the hospital, she had tried not to think of him.

When Tricia heard the sound of his footsteps in the hallway and saw the door to the room begin to open, her heart fluttered unreasonably, and she knew her efforts had been in vain.

Randall walked into the room with a brisk stride that spoke of efficiency, but when he saw Tricia he slowed noticeably. "I expected you on Wednesday," he said in a tone that she did not recognize and could not identify.

"I spent a few days with my aunt and uncle. I thought Emily would have told you."

"Whether or not Emily told me has nothing to do with it. You suffered an injury, Tricia, possibly serious," he said sternly. "I had a reason for saying I wanted to see you again in three days when I released you from the hospital. What if there had been complications while you were off visiting? I can't help you if you aren't cooperative."

"I was in Houston," she replied, unable to understand his irritation with her, "not in some third world country. There are doctors in Houston, you know. If I had had any problems, I would have called one of them. I have friends who are doctors there. They would have been happy to treat me if I had had any complications."

"All right," he said after a contemplative pause, "you have a point. But it is important for you to take care of yourself."

Tricia looked at him, amused at his seriousness. "I apologize if I've worried you."

He had been standing across the small room from her, but now he walked near. "Apology accepted, if you'll promise to follow my orders more closely in the future."

"I promise," she said, holding up her right hand as if taking an oath, smiling to combat his seriousness.

Her contagious smile affected him, and he too smiled. "Now, what was so important in Houston that you couldn't wait?"

Tricia hesitated before answering, the years of habit, evasiveness causing her to be less than honest. "Emily was making such a fuss over me that I felt guilty, especially when she already has so much to do. Raising four young active boys can't be easy."

Randall nodded thoughtfully as she spoke, then he stepped nearer to her. "But what's the real reason?"

Tricia froze momentarily, somewhat taken aback by his perceptiveness. "I had somewhere to go. Somewhere I go every Tuesday and Thursday. I didn't see why a bump on the head should stop me. My aunt and uncle go that way also, and you said not to drive, so I just stayed over with them. They came and picked me up Monday night, and I stayed until last night."

"Do you ever give anyone a straight answer?" he asked with annoyance apparent in his voice, beginning to believe that perhaps Bradley had been correct in surmising that there was a man in Tricia's life. He wondered if Tricia had gone to meet him at some prearranged place and time, not to her aunt and uncle's as she claimed.

"I'm just a private person," she said softly by way of explanation. Then noting his expression of disapproval, she sighed with resignation. "All right, I'll tell you. I take classes at the University of Houston two days a week. My uncle is a professor of literature there, and my aunt teaches in the music department. I really didn't want to miss my classes, and I felt that it would be easier on Aunt Barbara and Uncle Jim if I stayed over rather than making them drive back and forth more than necessary."

"A college student?" he asked, taken aback by her candid answer. "You are full of surprises. I wouldn't have guessed, but you are the right age to be a college student.'' He seemed to be genuinely pleased that she had confided at least this small truth to him.

Tricia looked at him without offering further comment, and so he continued.

"What's your major? No, let me guess.'' He studied her for a minute. "You like working with plants. Is it horticulture?''

"No,'' she answered, shaking her head, the blond waves reflecting the light.

"Hmm.'' He wrinkled his brow in concentration. Then remembering her house he asked, "Interior design?''

"Nope. Not even close.'' She smiled, her blue eyes sparkling with mischief, reminding him of a child enjoying a game of Twenty Questions.

"What then?''

"I'm not actually majoring in anything. I'm taking a couple of classes in creative writing. If things work out, I'll increase my load next semester, take more classes. Getting the house and yard right took so much of my time, I couldn't handle too much this semester.''

"A writer?'' he asked with interest. "You're a writer. Well, that does answer a few questions.''

Her face showed signs of apprehension as she looked at him. "Questions?''

"Let's face it,'' he said casually, "not every twenty-one-year-old college student lives alone in a house like yours. Your finances are none of my business, but it did seem rather odd that you don't have any obvious means of financial suppor ''

"What made you think it odd?''

"When you're hesitant to tell people things, sometimes they jump to erroneous conclusions. In a town as small as Asheville, people know a great deal about their neighbors. Your excessive reclusiveness causes people to gossip about you, to speculate on your motives."

"I am not a recluse," she objected, interrupting him. "I just don't think my . . . my . . ." she stuttered. "It's not anyone's business."

"Tricia," he said in a soothing voice. "I didn't mean to upset you. I apologize if I've invaded your privacy."

She looked up. The concern and sincerity in his voice were reflected in his eyes also, and her irritation faded, replaced by the old sorrow. The guilty feelings she had come here to escape. The past she had tried to forget. She wasn't unhappy with Randall. It was life in general. It was the inescapable fact that no one can go back in time, rearrange the events of the past, save the lives of the people they care for. "I inherited some money, and I earned the rest," she said meekly by way of an apology. Why was it every time she came in contact with Randall she ended up trading information about herself for forgiveness? she wondered. Why was appeasing him so important to her? "Now you know. There's no more mystery for you to wonder about."

"I see," he said softly, affected by the saddened overtones of her voice but not knowing how to comfort her. He felt a sudden urge to take her in his arms, bury his face in her soft, shining hair, and whisper words of consolation. He wondered if her hair smelled like wildflowers, if her skin would be soft and warm to his touch. An instinctive urge to protect her arose in him, but he pushed it away. Whatever secret she had been keeping, he now felt certain it was neither an affair nor a crime, but something she had buried deep within herself, some unwanted knowledge she sought to forget. Rather than continue and risk upsetting her further, he changed the subject. "I suppose it's time to get back to the reason you came here today. I'll call for my nurse, then we can get started."

"Such a nice girl." Mrs. Turner beamed. She was Randall's nurse, a robust woman of about sixty who took a grandmotherly interest in every patient. "Did you see the flowers she brought?"

"Flowers?" Randall asked.

"She came in with a huge bouquet of flowers. She said you had admired them in her yard. You should see how they brighten the waiting area, like a vase of sunshine."

"Hmm," Randall murmured absentmindedly. "A thoughtful gesture."

"Oh, yes, and they tell me that the residents at the nursing home simply adore her."

"Nursing home? What are you talking about?"

"Didn't you know? She visits the nursing home every Monday, plays the piano, and talks to the folks. Really cheers up the place."

"No. I didn't know," Randall said reflectively. "Though she told me she wanted to fit into the community, find a place for herself here."

"Well, she's certainly done that." Mrs. Turner paused, then asked in a serious tone, "Dr. Land, what is she doing here? This town doesn't have much to offer a young woman in the way of excitement, especially one who's beautiful, wealthy, and young.''

"From what I've been able to comprehend, she's searching for a gentler way of life, a way to turn back the clock to simpler times.''

"She did seem rather depressed today, as if she was on the verge of tears. Poor thing.'' Mrs. Turner stared thoughtfully at the door Tricia had walked through when she left. "Maybe she was the victim of some terrible crime. Maybe that's why she moved away from the city. Maybe the poor thing has been frightened.''

"I hadn't thought of that, Mrs. Turner,'' Randall answered, turning toward the same doorway she seemed to speak to, as if to ask a question of it. "Though to me she doesn't appear to be frightened, not frightened so much as saddened.''

"Well, it's your duty as her doctor to find out what the problem is. 'Treat the whole patient,' I always say.''

"Maybe I will,'' he remarked thoughtfully. "Maybe I will drop in on her some time.''

"Good for you, Dr. Land,'' she remarked approvingly.

A week passed before Randall saw Tricia again. It wasn't that he hadn't thought about her during those seven days. He pondered how he should go about dropping in on her. She obviously wanted her privacy respected, yet he also felt that there was some merit to what Mrs. Turner had said.

During the week he had dropped by to visit Emily and the boys three times, hoping that Tricia would be outside and he could casually wander over and inquire about her health.

Then one morning, jogging in the park, he found himself keeping watch on Tricia's house, wondering if she
was home and if she was awake. When he reached the
side of the park opposite her house, Randall crossed the
street, walked up the path, and rang her doorbell. While
he debated whether his impulsive actions had been wise,
Tricia opened the door.

"Morning, Tricia," he said cheerfully, noting with relief that despite the early hour she was already up and
dressed. She wore well-fitted slacks and a light sweater
of pastel colors that tempted him to reach out and touch
it, to test the texture and learn of softness. "You look
nice," he said by way of understatement.

"Hello, Randall," she answered, surprised at his
early-morning visit. "Come in. Would you like some
coffee?"

"Yes, thanks," he said, entering the door she had
opened for him, noting the light floral scent of her perfume. "Coffee would be great. I run first thing in the
morning, so I haven't had any yet."

"I can make you breakfast," she offered. "I haven't
eaten either."

With a gesture of agreement he followed her as she
started toward the kitchen. There he noticed books, a
notepad, purse, and keys set together on a countertop
near the door leading to the garage.

"You have classes today," he said, recalling that she
had told him she went into Houston every Tuesday and
Thursday.

"Yes, but not for a couple of hours. Do you like eggs?
I can make us a ham and cheese omelet and some French

toast,'' she said, beginning to take items from the refrigerator.

"If it's no trouble,'' he floundered, wondering what he would say if she asked why he had come.

"Not at all. Breakfast is the most important meal of the day, isn't it?'' she asked with good humor, remembering his stern warnings that she should eat correctly.

"Absolutely,'' he agreed, sitting at her small breakfast table, noting how comfortable she seemed in the gourmet kitchen. "You seem happier today.''

"I got an offer on a story I wrote. A publisher wants to include it in a short story anthology. I'm going to ask my professor his opinion on the offer. Hopefully it's a good one and I can sell the story.''

"Sell it?''

"Of course. That's why I'm studying writing. So I can earn an income.''

"But I thought you had inherited money,'' he asked in some confusion.

"I did inherit some money, but I spent almost all of it on the house. What's left won't last forever, and I'm not trained to do anything else. Not anything that I want to do at any rate.'' She added the last phrase as an afterthought.

"What about your old job? I seem to remember you said you had inherited some money and earned the rest.''

"I quit when I moved here,'' she answered, quickly dismissing the subject of her past work. "If I can learn to write well enough, I can write here and mail my work to publishers. That way I can be independent and self-supporting without having to sacrifice my private life to do so.''

"I see," he said, contemplating as she poured the egg mixture into the warmed pan and sprinkled cheese over it. "And is that what's important to you? Being able to finance your privacy?"

"I can't ask my aunt and uncle for money," she said, neatly avoiding the issue of privacy and addressing the question of economics. "And I'm *not* moving back to Houston. So I guess I'd say it's important as a means."

"Toward what end?"

Tricia thought for a moment. "I want to make my own decisions, for my life to be more than just the sum of the things that have happened to me in the past. I want to feel good about my life, my home, about what I do, the people I choose to spend time with, and the places I choose to go or not to go."

"All right then," he said, seizing the opportunity at hand. "Tomorrow is Emily's birthday. I'm planning to take her and Bradley out to celebrate. Will you come along?"

"Sure, I guess so," Tricia agreed before she realized that she had just accepted her first date since Steven died nearly a year ago. "Breakfast is ready."

"How did you decide on Asheville?" he asked with deliberate casualness as Tricia set the food on the table.

Tricia's forehead wrinkled, as if she were debating how to answer him. Then she shrugged her shoulders. "Aunt Barbara mentioned once that my mother and grandparents lived here for a short time when Mother was a teenager. She said that, looking back, it seemed that was the happiest time in my mother's life." Tricia fell silent for a moment, reflecting. "I guess there was something poetic about searching for the future in the past.'' Tricia sat in her chair. "Let's eat before it gets cold,'' she said, effectively closing the subject.

Over breakfast they talked about Tricia's writing.

"Your story, what's it about?''

"It's about a young man during the Civil War. He makes mistakes and blames himself for the defeat of his regiment and the deaths of the men in it. He then spends the rest of his life in a complex pattern, simultaneously hiding his guilt from others and atoning for what he perceives as his sins. The story is told through a series of flashbacks as the man, now old, lies dying.''

"Whew." He whistled softly. "What a complicated psychological profile for a character invented by a student writer. It sounds interesting. May I read it?''

Tricia hesitated. "I guess so. I have some extra copies. I'll get one for you. How's your food?''

"The breakfast is delicious,'' he said to her across the table. "How can it be that such a good cook stays so thin?''

"Now you're trying to flatter me,'' she said with a note of disapproval. She'd heard flattery, and she didn't trust it. She much preferred the truth, even if it wasn't complimentary.

"I never flatter,'' he defended himself. "I'm honest to a fault.''

Tricia studied his face, then deciding he was sincere, she answered. "I've enjoyed having someone to eat with.'' She thought of the meals she'd skipped just to avoid having to eat alone. "Maybe you'll consider jogging over again some morning.''

"Is that an invitation?'' he asked with mischief in his

voice. "Don't invite a bachelor to a wonderful meal like this unless you're sincere."

"I'm sincere," she said, though a note of uncertainty in her voice threatened to betray her. "I'm sincere to a fault," she added, echoing his statement.

As Tricia finished speaking she noticed Randall staring at her across the table, a curious smile playing on his lips. "What is it?"

"I was just thinking, Tricia, that you are like a jack-in-the-box. You stay tightly closed up. Then when I least expect it, you startle me by opening up, being honest, sincere, trusting. But just as quickly, you close up again, leaving me to crank away, hoping you'll open up again."

"Meaning?"

"Meaning I'd like to get to know you better, but sometimes when we talk, I feel as if you're answering all my questions without really giving out any information. You're like a turtle drawn up in its shell, just peeking out occasionally to see what's going on in the world outside, but afraid to come out and take part."

"I hadn't realized doctors were so full of similes and metaphors. Are you sure there isn't an English teacher lurking around somewhere inside of you?"

Randall smiled and shook his head, acknowledging to himself how aptly she had, once again, turned the conversation from herself.

After they had eaten, Tricia carried their dishes to the sink, and Randall followed. As she ran water over the plates the sunlight came through the window, reflecting on her golden hair.

"Your hair." Randall sighed softly, standing near her.

"What?" she asked, turning to face him. "Is something wrong with it?"

"It's incredible," he answered, reaching out and running his hand over its soft, thick texture. "Soft and shiny." He leaned toward her, his eyes glowing with appreciation. His hand was on the back of her head, and he gently pulled her toward him. His head bent forward to hers and then their lips met with the timidity of a first kiss. Tricia stood frozen with Randall's arms around her, and the look of innocence on her face that had caused him to want to kiss her was replaced by a blushing look of confusion.

"I have to go to school . . . now," she stammered.

"See you tomorrow night, Princess, seven o'clock," he said, releasing her from his embrace, picking up a copy of the story she'd written, and walking toward the doorway, a smile of self-satisfaction prominently displayed on his face.

The next day, Friday, Emily visited and excitedly offered to help Tricia choose her dress for dinner. "With all those boys and men around, it's nice to have someone to do girl things with for a change," she confided.

Tricia led the way up the stairs and opened a closet that held a sizable array of fashionable gowns. "Have at it," she said.

"Goodness, Tricia." She sighed. "Where did you get all these clothes?"

"My last job required that I dress."

"That's an understatement if I ever heard one," Emily replied.

"We probably should choose something simple if

we're going to eat someplace here in town,'' Tricia suggested.

At length Emily decided on a tea-length dress with a jacket, both a deep rose color. The strapless dress fit tightly at the bodice, but the skirt flared into fullness.

"Don't you think it's a bit much?" Tricia asked. "Randall might think I'm throwing myself at him."

"If Randall even notices," Emily said dismally, "he'll probably just remark on your bone structure. Sometimes it annoys me the way he's a doctor twenty-four hours a day. Ever since that disappointment with Corrie, he's thrown himself into his work."

Emily continued her remarks, but Tricia's mind vividly recalled his tentative kiss in her kitchen after breakfast and the reactions it had caused. "Sweaty palms!" she had muttered to herself in disgrace as she had driven toward Houston. "Sweaty palms, like a schoolgirl!"

"Tricia?"

"Yes, Emily. I was just thinking that maybe I should wear something more conservative."

"Nonsense. We can be conservative anytime." She paused. "If you're really concerned, just don't take off the jacket. But please wear the dress—you look too beautiful not to."

Chapter Four

Tricia dressed carefully. She curled her hair and applied her makeup with more attention than she had given her grooming in many months. She polished her nails and then chose her accessories: an elaborate, eye-catching necklace, dangling earrings, and hair combs of dazzling rhinestones. She studied her appearance in the mirror. Then, cautious that she might attract too much attention, she changed her jewelry for simpler items. A necklace of a single, brilliant, pear-shaped diamond lay on the creamy, smooth skin of her chest, and she put simple diamond studs into her pierced ears. The jewelry had been a gift from Steven last Christmas, only a few days before he died.

Shaking off the dreary memories, Tricia put on shoes that had been dyed to match her dress and grabbed her beaded handbag before turning off her light and walking downstairs.

Fifteen minutes before he arrives, she told herself. Then Tricia went to the piano to pick up the birthday gift she had chosen for Emily. Impulsively she sat down and began to play a melody. Tricia played with great expression. Her talent was unmistakable, and so was her training. Music had been the first interest Tricia had shared with her Aunt Barbara when she had come into her home and her life. It had become a bond between them. Barbara recognized and encouraged her niece's talent, and Tricia went on to win many awards for her musical abilities.

To Tricia, expressing herself through music had come easier than expressing herself verbally. She remembered as a child she'd had episodes of banging angrily on the piano keys, even when she didn't know why she felt the anger and frustration. Tonight Tricia's long, slender fingers traveled easily over the keys. Music, warm and passionate, filled the room.

The doorbell sounded, breaking the mental link that held Tricia to her piano, giving birth to her music. She rose from the piano, smoothed her skirt, and walked to the door to greet Randall.

As they entered the expensive French restaurant, Emily, Bradley, Tricia, and Randall were greeted warmly. The maître d' smiled. "Happy birthday, Emily. Your brother has made all the arrangements. Your table is ready." Then, noticing Tricia, he smiled. "Ah, Mademoiselle McGill, you have a different escort tonight. *Oui?*"

Tricia noticed Randall's raised eyebrows at this remark, and she answered, "*Oui,* Monsieur. Mr. Lindow
couldn't make it tonight."

"*C'est dommage.* But Dr. Land, he is your escort, and
younger than the other and more attractive." The maître d'
said this to Tricia in low tones and winked at her approvingly as he did so.

He then showed them to their table, wished them a
pleasant evening, and retired to greet the next group of
incoming guests.

Emily, Bradley, Tricia, and Randall sat together in the
soft lighting. In the background a small orchestra played
and in the next room couples danced to the mood-setting
music.

"So," Randall said lightheartedly, "you come here
regularly with Harry Lindow?"

"Every Monday for lunch," she answered. "Harry
introduced me to this restaurant. It's his favorite. He enjoys getting out, and he's wonderful company."

"That's so nice." Emily beamed approvingly. "Harry's
such an outgoing person. Now that he's healthy again, he
must enjoy your lunches together."

"We both do," Tricia answered sincerely, unaware of
how the candlelight softly lit her face and reflected in
her eyes against the dimness of the room, giving the
effect that she was surrounded by a mystical aura, that
she was not a person at all but a spirit. This fascinated
Randall, who sat across from her and gazed at her intently until Emily interrupted.

"It can't hurt him, can it, Randall?" Emily asked her
brother. "Just to get out and eat this delicious food once
a week?"

"Not at all," Randall agreed, tearing his eyes away from Tricia. "I'm sure these dates are a great boost to his ego."

"It's not that kind of a relationship." Tricia laughed at the idea of her lunches with Harry being misunderstood. "Since I met Harry, he's become like a grandfather to me."

"Are you sure he perceives the relationship in the same way?" Bradley asked cautiously.

"Absolutely. He told me I'm like the grandchild he's always wanted." Tricia contemplated, then asked, "Doesn't he have a grown son? Why is Harry so hungry for family?"

Emily and Bradley exchanged meaningful glances across the table.

"Although John is in his mid forties, he never married," Emily replied, carefully sidestepping the issue.

"Harry and his son don't see each other often," Randall explained. "They had a disagreement years ago, when I was still too young to understand the complications."

"Years ago?" Tricia echoed. "What could be so terrible to keep a family alienated for years?"

"When John was young, in his twenties, he did something Harry didn't approve of. I attempted to get them to reconcile when Harry was ill. Unfortunately I was unsuccessful. According to Harry, John refuses to live up to his responsibilities. According to John, Harry refuses to forgive him a youthful error." Randall paused. "That pretty well summarizes the situation. The details are, I suppose, private."

Despite her uneasiness over her discovery of Harry's

isolation from his son, Tricia enjoyed the leisurely dinner. She relaxed, feeling part of a group, and her three companions took Tricia into their easy confidence. The evening progressed without a hint of awkwardness. Even Emily refrained from subtle hints about a relationship between her brother and the woman who just now seemed to fascinate him.

"Tricia," Randall said to her after they had eaten, "Would you like to dance?"

"Dance?" Tricia asked, looking around at the dance floor. "Yes. I'd like that."

Randall rose from his seat and pulled back Tricia's chair for her. He took her hand and led her toward the next room. There, with the soft music surrounding them, Randall turned toward her, paused briefly, then reached out for her.

Tricia went into Randall's strong arms, and she soon realized how comfortable she felt with her head against his broad chest, her body held firmly to his. Relaxing, she closed her eyes, the movements of her body instinctively following Randall's.

"I enjoyed having breakfast with you again this morning." Randall smiled down at the enticing woman in his arms, wondering about his chances of making it three breakfasts in a row.

Tricia smiled up at him. "Yes, it was fun. Especially watching you do the dishes."

"It was my turn, besides I wouldn't want you to get dishpan hands on my account."

Randall had learned that Tricia was warm and responsive as long as he kept everything in the present tense. It was when he inquired about the past that she withdrew.

Maybe in time, he thought. *But tonight we'll stick to her ground rules.* "Emily tells me you're giving piano lessons to three of my four rambunctious nephews. I must say I admire your spunk. That's something I'd never attempt."

Tricia laughed. "You make it sound like a qualification for sainthood." Tricia thought of how she looked forward to the visit of each small boy, how they disturbed the emptiness and loneliness. "I really do enjoy them."

"You're amazing."

Tricia glanced at him doubtfully.

"Really, Tricia. You're beautiful, intelligent, and determined. You like old people and little children. You can cook, decorate a home like a showplace, and grow any flower known to mankind. You're full of contradictions and surprises."

Tricia observed Randall as he spoke, her face soft and expressionless. Did he really mean all he said? Then she looked away.

"And you dance very well," he murmured smoothly into her fragrant hair.

"Thank you." She sighed, her eyes moving upward to his face. "You're an excellent partner."

"I'd like to dance with you every day," he said tenderly.

In his arms, Tricia stumbled slightly, taken aback by the intimate nature of his remark. "Let's just dance," she said. "Let's not ruin this beautiful evening by making commitments that one of us can't or won't want to live up to."

They continued to dance together, Tricia close to

Randall. He thought of her uneasy rejection of his invitation to start a relationship, not surprised or put off by her refusal. Tricia was an interesting woman—a person in metamorphosis. He wasn't sure what she was changing from or what she would change into, but he sensed that she stood before a deep, narrow chasm, fearfully stepping from one side to the other.

"Are you angry?" Tricia asked, tentatively observing his solemn expression.

"Angry? No, not at all. My mind was somewhere else."

Tricia couldn't help but wonder if his mind was on *someone* else as he held her.

Randall's voice ended those thoughts. "I was thinking of what a contradiction you are. One moment you're dressed as if you want to be a wallflower, to go unnoticed. But tonight, well, let it suffice to say that every man who sees you is struck dumb."

"You're embarrassing me," Tricia whispered, modestly looking away and breaking the contact with him.

Randall gently pulled her back. He liked the scent that he'd come to associate with her and her soft voice as it curled up inside his ear. But she'd implied she wasn't ready to commit to a relationship. He'd give her the security of a little emotional distance. "What did your teacher think of your story? The one you gave me a copy of yesterday at breakfast," he asked.

"He's having a literary agent, a friend of his, look over the contract for me. He's very optimistic about it, however. He's even offered to make suggestions for the scenes they want rewritten."

"Then if the contract is good and you do the rewrites successfully, you'll be able to sell it?"

"Um-hum," she murmured as they danced.

"I'm glad for you, Tricia. I'm glad for Asheville. It would be a loss to this town if you weren't successful and moved back to Houston. You do a lot for the scenery here, you know." He paused. "You'll continue writing, won't you?"

"I guess so," she said softly, then she looked into Randall's face, so near hers, and she felt for a moment as if they were the only two people in the room. She liked the feeling, even if she didn't quite understand it. "Right now I don't even care. It's hard to think about careers and economics when the music is so lovely. After all, money isn't really so important, is it? As the old saying goes, it can't buy happiness."

He raised his eyebrows questioningly. "Do you really believe that?"

"Of course."

"My, you are naive," he answered condenscendingly.

This time it was Tricia who looked puzzled. She had known plenty of wealthy people who weren't happy. "What do you mean?"

"Anyone whose philosophy about money is that simple has never stared into the face of poverty." He paused before continuing. "You haven't worked in a charity hospital, seen the desperation in the eyes of parents who bring in children whose illnesses have grown steadily worse because they couldn't afford medical attention when the child first became ill. The hopelessness."

Randall paused again, then added cynically, "Maybe

money can't ensure happiness, but there are certain demons it can keep away.''

Tricia considered Randall thoughtfully, wondering about the private demons that haunted him. The expression in her eyes grew serious as she contemplated Randall's words and tried to fathom the experiences he must have gone through in developing this philosophy.

''Sorry, Princess,'' he said, returning to the tender charm that had characterized him through the evening. ''Tonight's not the time, and this isn't the place, to discuss the ills of our society.''

''Don't apologize,'' she whispered. ''I want to know all about you, how you think, how you feel, why you act the way you do.''

Randall smiled. ''But your eyes tell me everything you are thinking, and when you are dancing with me I want them to tell me something other than the fact that you are sympathetic.''

''I enjoyed this evening,'' Tricia said honestly as they walked into her house. She touched a small lamp in the entryway, bathing the room in soft, shadowy light. ''The food, the company, everything was wonderful. What a delightful escape from reality. Thank you.''

He considered her words, watching her walk from the entryway into the living area. ''You don't go out often, do you?'' he asked, thinking how Tricia had imprisoned herself just as the princess in the fairy tale had been held in a tower. He felt like the prince who called to Rapunzel to let down her hair. Tricia, indeed, needed to let down her hair.

''No, not on dates.''

"Why not?" he asked.

"I don't know," she answered, reflecting. "Because I'm a quiet, rather private person, I suppose. And I've always discouraged well-meaning people from setting up dates for me with friends, relatives, and so forth. They don't work out well and then it's awkward for everyone. I don't visit the bars and clubs where some single women go. I'm not comfortable with that swinging singles concept." She paused, reflecting, then continued. "But even when I was young in school, boys didn't ask me out much."

His eyes traveled over her. "I can understand that."

"What do you mean?" she asked defensively, turning to face him. In the near darkness of her living room, she could just barely read his features.

"Just take a look at yourself. No seventeen- or eighteen-year-old could summon the courage to ask out a . . . a goddess. I'm thirty-five, and at times when I look at you I feel rather like a commoner trying to gain the attentions of the king's daughter."

"Do you mean that?" she asked, biting her lower lip apprehensively.

"Princess, do you always bite your lip that way when you're nervous?" he asked, his fingers lightly touching her chin just below her mouth.

Tricia smiled uncertainly but did not answer.

"I saw you do that earlier in the hospital, and you're doing it again." He paused briefly, and lightly brushed her lips with the finger that had caressed her chin. "It's rather an odd thing about you, Tricia. You're always so evasive about what you say, so careful not to give out too much information, to keep everyone guessing at what you're thinking, how you feel. Yet your gestures give you away. Your hands are extremely expressive, and so are your eyes.''

''Did you mean what you said earlier? When you said that the reason boys didn't ask me out in school was because my physical appearance was intimidating?''

''Absolutely. And tonight, that dress! The color is perfect for you. It brings out the fairness of your skin and hair, your delicate beauty. You look more like an artist's creation, a porcelain doll, than a real woman. When we first went to dance this evening, I was afraid to touch you, afraid you'd disappear, like a mirage.''

Tricia stood without speaking for a few moments, considering. This kind, intelligent, and attractive man was wooing her with his words. Some kind of response was definitely in order. She wished she'd had more experience in these matters. ''I like you, Randall.'' It wasn't exactly a confession of undying love, but for Tricia it was a beginning, a tentative reaching out, and Randall understood.

''Good. Because I'm finding out more clearly every minute that I'm crazy about you. I haven't been able to get you out of my mind since the day I met you, the day Matthew hit your lovely head with his baseball. I watched you lying in that hospital bed, unconscious, and I was spellbound. I couldn't tear my eyes away. I kept wondering what you were like, why fate had arranged our meeting. Then the next morning, when you spoke to me, I felt there was such sadness in you. I couldn't help but wonder what had caused it. The mystery got to me. I couldn't help thinking about you, wondering.''

"There's nothing," she assured him. "There's nothing mysterious about me."

"So you keep telling me," Randall said with an easy, unconscious smile turning up the corners of his mouth. He took a step closer to her, so that they were almost touching. "But I don't believe you. I didn't believe it that morning in the hospital, the first time you told me, and I don't believe it now. In fact, I'm even more sure of it now. I think I'm going to have to spend time with you, get to know you, discover the answer to this riddle for myself."

"Spend time with me?"

"Yes," he whispered. "You're the one who likes mythology. I guess I may as well admit that I've been struck by Cupid's arrow."

"But Emily said you were dedicated to your profession," she objected. "She said you didn't have time for anyone or anything else."

"So Emily's been trying to interest you in me, huh? She just can't stand to see anyone not happily married and knee-deep in children like she and Bradley are. What else did she tell you?"

"Not much. Only that a girl named Corrie broke your heart and so you hide behind your dedication to your patients."

"Very dramatic. Emily did a good job with that story."

"You mean you aren't? You don't?"

"I was infatuated with Corrie for a short time when I was young. Too young," he emphasized. "It wasn't love. There wasn't anything to love. She was attractive, but brainless and shallow. I got over Corrie."

"But Emily said you don't date."

"I do date. I just don't report in to her, and, as a rule, I don't date women in this town. It seems almost unethical to date someone who may be a patient, someone I may have to treat for a medical problem. The roles could get confused. I could lose professional objectivity if I ever allowed myself to become emotionally involved. It's rather like the rule that doctors won't treat their own families."

"But I'm a patient of yours," she protested.

"There are exceptions to every rule," he murmured, drawing her close to him, close enough to smell her light perfume, to feel her breath fan him as she exhaled. "Besides, you made it clear that you knew other doctors." Randall ran his hands over her long, soft hair, then allowed them to rest around her narrow waist. "If you ever cut yourself with a kitchen knife, or get stung by a bee in those flowers of yours, or burn your hand while cooking, you come by my office and I'll fix you up. But if you have anything more serious than that, go to one of those other doctors you were talking about."

"No one else could ever be like you," she whispered shyly, resting her head against his broad, hard chest. The wave of feeling gathering strength inside her was quite unlike anything she had ever experienced. Without knowing why, she felt unable to move away from him, powerless to resist him. With a feeling of awe, Tricia realized that she wanted to be near Randall. The fresh air in small towns certainly did have some strange side effects.

Randall's lips came down on hers, and his hands, al-

ready around her waist, firmly pulled her down next to
him on the sofa.

Tricia found herself returning his kisses, but these
were new feelings to her. New, unexpected, and a little
frightening in their enormity.

"Tricia," he whispered huskily. "Tricia."

Tricia lifted her arms to wrap them around Randall's
neck, and closing her eyes, she gave in to his kisses.

Clinging together in the near darkness of the room, for
the first time in her life, Tricia became totally unaware
of place or time. There was no past to be ashamed of,
no future to fear. All that existed was the moment. Her
lids fell slowly over her eyes, closing out the real world,
a world of choices and consequences, making the emotional world she was quickly becoming a part of the only
one that existed. Her heart beat rapidly. More side effects
of the fresh air? she wondered.

"Mmmmm," Randall teased approvingly. "I like
kissing you."

Tricia suddenly felt like an inexperienced schoolgirl.
A blush rose to her face, and she inched away from him.

"Don't be embarrassed," he whispered in a tender
tone.

"Oh, Randall." She sighed. "I don't know what to
say."

"Don't say anything," he instructed, kissing the top
of her nose. His lips caressed hers while her heartbeat
increased, and she returned to the world that existed only
in his arms.

Suddenly the silence of the house was shattered by the
ringing of the telephone.

Tricia glanced toward it with a startled cry.

"Don't answer it," he advised.

"It could be an emergency," she answered, logic winning a feeble victory. After a moment of hesitation and another shrill, unwelcomed ring, Tricia rose unsteadily from the sofa and grabbed the telephone.

"Hello?" she answered.

A pause followed. Then Tricia turned her face toward Randall. "It's for you. Mrs. Simms has gone into labor. They need you at the hospital."

"Darn," he muttered, taking the phone from her.

"This is Dr. Land," he said without enthusiasm into the receiver.

A brief conversation followed, none of which Tricia could later remember, then he hung up the phone. "Tricia, I'm sorry, but I have to go."

"Will it take long?"

"I never know. These things can go very fast, or they can go on for hours, maybe all night."

"I understand," she lied.

"That's the way things happen in a doctor's life," he explained. "Good night, Tricia." He gathered her into his arms for a last, overwhelming, good-night kiss, then he turned to go. "Be sure you lock your door, Princess," he called out over his shoulder.

Tricia stood frozen, watching him moving away from her, seeing him disappear through the doorway. Then, slowly, the fog of happiness began to evaporate.

It seemed Tricia had just gotten into bed and closed her eyes when the telephone sounded for the second time that night. She reached for it in the darkness.

"Hello," she murmured sleepily.

"Tricia? This is Randall. You were sleeping, weren't you?"

"Randall? Is something wrong?"

"No. Nothing's wrong. I wanted to apologize for leaving in such a hurry. It was quite an ungentlemanly thing to do."

"I know you had to go."

"Yes. But my mind keeps conjuring this vision of you, standing in the doorway all alone."

Tricia remembered the scene, but she said nothing.

"You're not still standing there, are you?"

"No," she answered. "Of course not. I'm in bed."

"I love the sleepy sound of your voice."

"How's Mrs. Simms?"

"She's fine. She had a beautiful baby girl. Round and pink, a healthy baby with a full head of dark hair and big blue eyes."

"A baby girl," Tricia remarked a little dreamily.

"What's that I hear in your voice?" he asked in amusement.

"I don't know. I was just thinking of that tiny baby girl, of dressing her in ruffled dresses and putting tiny bows in her hair."

"Yes?" he asked, encouraging her to continue.

"Nothing. I guess I've been around Emily's boys so much that I haven't thought about little girls in a long time."

"And you? What do you want? Boys or girls, or some of each?"

"Me?" Tricia asked in surprise.

"Yes, you."

"I never thought about having children. I don't know if I'd be a good mother."

"Why?"

"I might make mistakes."

"Then get a puppy and practice."

"I was serious."

"Tricia, so am I. Everybody makes mistakes. As far as I've been able to observe, the mistakes parents make fall into two categories. Some people make mistakes because they love their children too much, they hold on too tight, do too much for their children. The other category is those parents who don't love their children enough, who don't do enough for them."

"It sounds so dismal. Perhaps I shouldn't even attempt it."

"But you should. You should have several children. All girls who look just like you."

"Why?"

"Well, if for no other reason than to pass your life on to the next generation. Tricia, it would be a shame to waste your beauty, your warmth, your loving nature."

"Waste?" she asked in confusion.

"Yes. Wasted beauty, wasted warmth, wasted love."

"Why are you saying these things?"

He paused before answering. "Probably just because it's four-thirty in the morning and I haven't had any sleep yet. Because tonight I felt something I haven't felt in years. Because I feel like I'm watching a beautiful woman blossom from a cold, mysterious flower right before my eyes. Because I think I'm fall—"

"Randall, Randall," she interrupted. "Get some sleep. Do you have patients coming in the morning?"

"Yes. At ten."

"Then go to bed. Get some sleep, a few hours anyway."

"Good night, Tricia."

"Good night, Randall." She hung up the phone and lay back on her pillows, but she was unable to sleep.

Chapter Five

Sometimes it seemed to Tricia that she had spent the first twenty years of her life without ever having made an important decision on her own. She'd simply gone along with the suggestions, ideas, and recommendations of others. When, at last, she had struggled free of the protective cocoon that had shielded her for so long then suddenly threatened to smother her, Tricia was faced with a myriad of decisions, and right or wrong, she'd made daring choices. In less than a year she had quit her job, bought and oversaw the remodeling of a house, moved to a town where she didn't know even one person, and enrolled in college courses.

Sitting comfortably in the atrium-style patio of her home, curled up in her fan-back wicker chair and gratefully absorbing the last warmth of the autumn evening sun, Tricia acknowledged that by far the most confusing thoughts were the ones she now struggled with. After the initial, overwhelming experience of being swept up into a storm of feelings for Randall, Tricia felt that she must give some thought to their relationship.

She recalled the night of Emily's birthday with a warm rush of color to her face. What had come over her? she wondered. Kissing Randall the first evening they spent together was not wise, she admitted to herself, and it certainly wasn't the way to build a relationship based on respect. There was no denying her intense attraction to Randall, but she wasn't ready for a physical relationship.

Tricia watched the sun slowly slip behind the trees that stood on the horizon, hoping she could find a way to make Randall understand without alienating him.

As dusk gathered in the neighborhood, Tricia crossed her arms and curled her legs up under her, a contented ball of warmth against the rapidly cooling world. She closed her eyes and listened to the tune of the darkness falling on the town. Crickets and frogs began their serenade, foretelling the appearance of the moon and stars in the ebony sky. Their harmony with the world was infectious, and Tricia was grateful to be a part of it, however hidden and insignificant. *Small town, USA,* Tricia thought appreciatively.

The night air carried the sound of dried leaves driven by a careless wind, rustling along the ground, the muffled voices of neighbors, and the music of a radio several houses away. From the distance, drawing nearer, came the sound of a car driving slowly along the street, followed by a brief silence, then the closing of a car door. *Someone getting home late from work,* Tricia thought idly.

The ringing of the doorbell brought Tricia from her reveries, and she rose slowly on stiffened limbs to answer its summons.

"Hi, Tricia." Randall smiled his unexpected greeting.

"Come in," Tricia invited, gesturing inside.

Randall entered, bending slightly to place a kiss on her cheek. "I hope you don't mind my stopping by without calling first."

"Of course not." Tricia's smile confirmed her pleasure in his visit and she motioned him toward the sofa. "Would you like a drink?"

"Yes," he answered wearily. "It's been a nerve-racking day."

Tricia poured Randall a glass of wine and sat next to him. "Things hectic at the office?"

He placed his arm loosely around her shoulder. "Enough to remind me that I owe myself a vacation."

Something in the tone of his voice told Tricia that Randall was serious, not simply talking out his frustrations.

"How long will you be gone?" she asked, acknowledging that although she hadn't known him long, she'd miss him.

Randall turned toward her, a devilish look in his eyes. "You mean how long will *we* be gone."

"We?" she asked, her eyes widening with surprise and distress.

"We're leaving Thursday after your classes and returning late Monday—a long weekend trip to Vicksburg, Mississippi." He smiled with self-satisfaction.

"Vicksburg?" Tricia asked. "What are you talking about?"

"The story you're writing is about the Civil War, isn't it?"

"Yes."

"There's a wonderful Civil War battleground there. The history almost comes alive. It will be great research for your story."

Tricia was stunned. Randall was offering to take her to Vicksburg in order to help her with her story. The joy that thought gave her was diminished by a shadow of doubt.

Randall noticed her hesitation. "You'll come, won't you? It took some doing, but I've convinced a doctor friend to cover emergencies for me."

"Randall." Her eyes sought his. "I'd love to go to Vicksburg. . . . "

"Then why do I feel there's a *but* coming in your next statement?"

"We need to get something settled," she began with more confidence than she felt.

"Yes," he agreed. "It seems last time we were together I had to leave in a rush."

"Yes," Tricia whispered shyly, looking down at her hands. "Now that I've had time to think about it, to detach myself from the situation, I'm afraid my behavior may have given you the wrong impression. That wasn't me. I've never acted that way. And now . . . oh, Randall . . . going away together for four days and nights. . . . I don't know."

Randall gave her a wide, knowing smile. "If that's what you're worried about, relax. We're going to be well chaperoned."

Tricia looked at him quizzically. What was the man talking about?

"Your writing and my schedule aren't my only motivations, Tricia," he admitted.

"What else?"

"The other night at dinner, when you talked about your lunches with Harry, I was thinking about how much it helps him to get out occasionally. He does need to get out. He hasn't gone anywhere outside Asheville since his heart attack a year ago."

"Harry's going with us?" Tricia asked with obvious approval, her doubts about the trip evaporating in the bright light of her happiness now that her problem was solved.

"Harry will be there, so we'll have separate rooms," he said. "And on Saturday he's visiting an old war buddy who lives in Vicksburg."

"I guess that's fine," she mused aloud.

"Second thoughts, Princess?" His large hands took her face and held it gently so their eyes met.

"Not about the trip," she answered, realizing how much she did want to go, to see Vicksburg, yes, but more to spend time with Randall, to get to know him and enjoy him.

"About this?" he asked huskily, his lips touching hers.

"Not . . . not that . . . exactly," Tricia whispered in an unsteady voice after his lips had done their best to confuse her.

"Then we'll just take it slowly," he promised, his lips teasing the outline of her mouth. "One step at a time." The kiss that followed his words was surprisingly gentle, assuring her of his earnest desire to do what his words promised.

"Have you had dinner yet, Randall?" Tricia asked, running her fingers through his light brown hair. "I can cook more than just breakfast, you know."

"I'd love to, Princess, but I can't."

Tricia tried to hide her disappointment. "It's okay, Randall. We'll do it another time."

"It's just that I've already committed myself."

"You don't have to explain to me," Tricia said meekly, not wanting to know he had a date with someone else. "You have the right—"

"Tricia," Randall said, reading the emotion in her face. "I'm nephew-sitting next door."

Relief flooded through her. "Baby-sitting?" She threw her arms around Randall with such force that it almost knocked him off balance.

Laughing, Randall lifted Tricia into his arms then arranged himself on the sofa with her on his lap. "Try not to be so happy about it. You're not the one stuck with the four boys all evening."

"Randall," she cried. "What a perfect idea! We can do it together. Kind of even up the odds. What do you say?"

"I say you're crazy to volunteer, but if you're willing, then let's go."

Five hours later Tricia knew why Randall thought she was crazy to volunteer. "Just how did you sucker me into this?" she asked with weary satisfaction as she picked up the last of the toys in the den.

"You thought I had a date with someone else." Randall winked at her over an armload of toys. "You came just to make sure I didn't."

"Don't you ever get tired of being right?" she asked playfully as she dropped her load into the toy box and held the lid open for Randall to follow her lead.

"Never," he said, depositing the toys then sitting on the lid to make sure it closed. "Just call me Mr. Right."

"Well, Mr. Right, how did we do?" she asked over her shoulder, heading for the kitchen to do the last of the dishes. "I've never baby-sat before."

Randall stopped, unbelieving. "You've never baby-sat?"

"Nope." She shook her head. "I don't have any nieces, nephews, or cousins. Aunt Barbara and Uncle Jim's friends didn't have children. This is new to me."

"You definitely passed your test," he answered, following her into the kitchen. "You acted like a real pro. Where did you learn to cook hot dogs and play hide-and-seek?"

Tricia turned to Randall. "I'm inexperienced," she said with a mischievous grin, "not stupid. I can improvise."

"Is that so?" Randall asked with a slow smile.

Just at that moment Marty began to cry. Not a whimpering it-might-go-away cry, but a full-force, top-of-the-lungs outburst.

Randall eyed the stairs warily. "It was probably your choice of bedtime stories," he remarked, putting his arm around Tricia's waist as they started up the stairs.

"Cyclops a little too gory for the baby?" she asked as she lifted Marty from his crib.

"Actually, I thought it was just right for this bloodthirsty crew, but maybe the little guy here hasn't graduated from Hans Christian Andersen yet.''

''Fairy tales?'' Tricia asked as she rocked the quieted child against her. ''I don't know any.''

Randall stared at Tricia. There was no reason not to believe her. Obviously the checkered past she tried to hide from him contained more dark than light squares. ''The princess marries the prince. They live happily ever after.''

Tricia smiled at him. ''Thanks, you've saved me a lot of worry.''

An hour later Bradley opened the front door, quickly surveyed the quiet room, and put his finger to his lips in a gesture of silence to Emily. There on the sofa in the dim light, Marty, Tricia, and Randall sat snuggled together and sound asleep.

''What a picture!'' Emily whispered. ''I told you they'd be perfect together.''

When Tricia returned home from school on Tuesday afternoon, she noticed Matthew sitting alone under a tree in his yard. Usually exuberant and lively, he seemed sullen and pensive.

Tricia walked across her lawn and sat on the grass beside him. ''What's wrong, Matthew?'' she asked, ruffling his hair.

''Nothin','' he said, though his voice and gestures contradicted his statement. He idly plucked a blade of grass and then released it to the wind.

''In trouble with your mom?''

''Nope,'' he answered.

Silence. Finally, just as Tricia was beginning to think

herself a failure in the area of juvenile communication, he began to talk again. "Uncle Randall promised to take me fishing this weekend, because next week is my birthday," he said with great disappointment evident in his voice. "We go every year on the weekend before my birthday."

"And now he's not," Tricia concluded, immediately seeing the problem.

"Instead he's taking you and Mr. Lindow to Vicksburg."

Tricia's heart went out to Matthew. She knew firsthand the pain of unkept promises and the loneliness of childhood. "Aren't there places to fish in Vicksburg?" she asked.

Matthew turned to her, uncomprehending. "Of course there are," he said impatiently. "But I'm not going to be there."

"Of course you are, Matthew," she said confidently. "A trip to Vicksburg will be my birthday gift to you."

The ferocity of the hug that followed her words caught Tricia off guard and literally knocked her to the ground.

"Do you mean it?" Matthew asked, his cares forgotten as they sprawled on the lawn.

"I'll talk to Randall and to your mom tonight," she assured him as she regained an upright position and began to pick fallen leaves from her hair.

"You're the greatest!"

When Tricia explained the seventy-pound planned addition to her luggage to Randall that night, he simply sighed good-naturedly. "There goes Saturday night." He feigned disappointment. "Instead of lobster and wine, it'll be lollipops and Walt Disney." Then he pulled Tricia to him, complimented by her interest in keeping his reputation with his nephew intact. "But he rides in the back with Harry, and he sleeps in your room."

"You've got yourself a deal, mister." Tricia smiled, grateful for his understanding of her impulsive action.

"Are you sure you're ready to be a weekend parent?" he asked.

"I guess I am," she answered solemnly, remembering Matthew's face when she first sat next to him. "I felt the labor pains this afternoon."

By noon on Thursday the happy foursome was heading east on Interstate Highway Ten toward Mississippi. Emily had been hesitant about letting Matthew go, but Randall had finally convinced her that missing two days of school would hardly be fatal to Matthew's first-grade education. With a wink at his son, Bradley added his opinion that the trip would be educational. The happy truant was now engaged in a game of Chinese checkers with Harry in the backseat of Randall's car.

Tricia read aloud from brochures she'd picked up at the travel agency where she'd made the hotel reservations. Before they reached Baton Rouge, where they would stop for dinner, it had been decided that they'd spend Friday touring Vicksburg National Military Park and Sunday sight-seeing in downtown Vicksburg. Saturday was, of course, reserved for fishing and a picnic.

Harry expressed regret that the cool weather prohibited a trip to the commercial water park in nearby Jacksonville, saying that "pretty young things in bikinis" were what he needed to get his "old ticker" going again.

After eating a meal of fresh Gulf seafood blackened and heavily spiced Cajun style, they left Interstate Ten and took Highway Sixty-one north to Vicksburg. By the time they arrived, both Harry and Matthew were snoring in the backseat. Inspired by the light, cheerful conversation of the day and frequent stops at McDonald's, Tricia was acquiring the feeling of a real family vacation.

At the hotel, a bellboy carried everyone's luggage to their rooms. Randall followed, holding a sleeping Matthew in his arms. To an unknowing onlooker, the group could have been a happy family—grandfather, father, mother, and sleeping son. Tricia warmed to the thought. The only sign that the little group was not what it appeared to be was the instructions to the bellboy to put Randall's and Harry's bags in one room, and Tricia's and Matthew's in another.

Harry wished Tricia pleasant dreams and disappeared into his room in search of a warm, soft bed.

Randall followed Tricia into her room and laid his sleeping nephew on one of the beds as soon as Tricia had drawn back the covers and plumped the pillows.

"Whew!" Randall sighed, flexing his arms. "He's getting heavy."

Tricia watched Matthew settle himself more comfortably between the covers. As she bent over him, lightly-stroking his sleeping features, she wondered vaguely if she'd do the same for her own child someday.

"They look so peaceful when they're asleep," Randall said, thinking of the rambunctious antics of his oldest nephew during his waking hours.

"Now, Randall," Tricia scolded mildly, "you can't be that cynical. I know you enjoyed him today."

"I enjoyed everything about today," Randall agreed. "Matthew's knock-knock jokes, Harry's war stories, and especially you." Randall glanced around the room, noting the sleeping child. He gestured to the door that led out to the balcony. "Let's step out, okay? See if there are any stars tonight?"

Tricia smiled her agreement, not willing to have Randall leave her so soon. He took her hand and led her into the frosty night air.

"Thanks for coming, Tricia," Randall murmured, wrapping his arms around her against the cold. "It means a lot to me. Even if we had to turn around and go back home right now, today was worth the trip—just being with you, near you, hearing you laugh and sing those silly songs with Matthew."

Tricia snuggled more closely against him. "I'm glad I came."

For endless moments they stood together, looking out over the sleepy city, then Randall spoke in a hushed tone of longing. "I'd like to kiss you, Tricia."

"But Matthew's asleep just a few feet away," she reminded him in an unsteady whisper.

"And it's already past midnight," he added, trying to convince himself.

"And we have a busy day ahead of us tomorrow."

"Maybe we should just say good night," Randall suggested, but neither of them moved.

"Yes, that's probably the best thing," she finally agreed unenthusiastically. With great reluctance she stepped away from him, but with a quick, determined step he bridged the distance she had created between them and pulled her into his arms. His lips brushed hers in a kiss so tender, Tricia felt as light and free as a falling star.

"Good night, Tricia," he said suddenly, releasing her. "I'll see you in the morning." He walked rapidly inside.

Still stunned from the emotion of his kiss, Tricia stood on the balcony a moment longer, her thoughts reeling.

Friday morning dawned clear and bright, a perfect November day. Wearing jeans and sweat shirts, the party set out for a day of researching Civil War history at the site of one of the most famous battles of that war, now a seventeen hundred–acre military park. Tricia brought along a pen and notepad to jot down inspiring tidbits of information.

Harry seemed most impressed with the miles of now grass-covered trenches that had been dug by the soldiers for protection during the long battle. He walked out the route of the Northern troops, who had dug line after line of protective trenches as they advanced against the Southerners during the forty-seven-day seige to capture the "Gibraltar of the Confederacy."

Matthew scoured the gift shop for toy guns, swords, and a Confederate flag, after which he felt himself prepared to do battle with the ghost of any Yankee soldier who may still lurk about the park.

Tricia was fascinated by the story of a Confederate woman who had refused to leave her home when ordered to do so "for her own protection" by Yankee officers. When the fighting grew fierce and the wooden exterior of the walls proved unable to stop the bullets that ricocheted through the house, the woman and her child were forced to seek safety in the only means available to them.

They stood inside the brick fireplace of the house for three days until the fighting receded. After that harrowing experience, the woman was more easily convinced to relocate, and the home was used by Northern troops as a division headquarters.

Randall was struck with the futility and horror of a war in which thousands of people died because of the lack of medical supplies and knowledge.

So fascinated was Tricia in all she saw and heard that she lost touch with time and her cares. She never noticed how often Randall took her hand in his as they walked together, reading inscriptions on the monuments. It felt completely natural when he slipped his arm around her waist and she leaned against him. She smiled as he brushed away the tears that formed in her eyes as they walked through the cemetery where uncountable headstones marked the final resting place of men and boys who had never returned home to their families either in life or in death.

So natural was this reaching out that neither Tricia nor Randall noticed, but the familiarity did not escape the notice of Randall's sharp-eyed nephew or his weekend grandfather, Harry.

When the sun set, darkening the battleground, the group made their way from the solemn graveyard back to Randall's car, feeling rather like weary time travelers stepping one hundred and twenty-five years through history.

They returned to the hotel to freshen up and change for dinner.

''I feel as if I should be dressed in a Southern belle's traditional gown and bonnet,'' Tricia said.

"Well, ma'am," Randall drawled, giving the Southern speech an accent even Robert E. Lee himself would envy. "Ah do declah, ya look as lovely as a magnolia blossom in the springtime dressed just like y'are." He kissed her hand in the affected style of century-old Southern chivalry.

Matthew, given a new zest for life by a short nap, once again brandished his sword and roamed the hallway in search of Yankees.

"Has anyone told little Jefferson Davis there that we lost that war?" Harry inquired.

They drove to a lovely pre–Civil War mansion, circa 1830, that was now a restaurant. The home still boasted a wide curved staircase, antique furnishings, and beautiful patterned gardens. At Matthew's request, they were seated near a crackling fireplace and a window overlooking the Mississippi River. As they feasted on Southern cuisine and discussed the events of the day, a waiter approached, asking Tricia and Randall if their "son" would like a complimentary slice of Mississippi mud cake and a souvenir Confederate flag.

Matthew, collapsing in giggles, managed to set the waiter straight. "I'm not their son. They're not even married yet! They're just in love." He did, however, consume the rich dessert and add the flag to his rapidly growing collection of Southern paraphernalia.

On the way back to the hotel Matthew once again succumbed to the exertion and adventures of the day and fell fast asleep, requiring Randall, once again, to carry him up to Tricia's room.

"I'm going to have a build like Arnold Schwarzenegger by the time we get home Monday evening if this keeps up," Randall complained mildly as he and Tricia once again settled their sleeping charge into his bed. They stood gazing down at the little boy.

Tricia moved closer to Randall. "Thank you for this weekend, Randall," she whispered. "It's been wonderful. Matthew is having a grand time being a truant from school. Harry's more animated than I've ever seen him."

"And you, Princess?" he inquired.

"I'm having the time of my life." Tricia smiled. "Though I have to admit I've never been mistaken for the mother of a seven-year-old before tonight." She paused, recalling the waiter's mistake and Matthew's reaction. After a pause she added, "It was kind of nice though, being mistaken for part of a real family. That's never happened to me before."

The slight edge of pain that shadowed her voice warned Randall that the earlier, playful mood had begun to slip. That Tricia was in danger of falling back into the shell of mystery and isolation she'd wrapped around herself earlier in their relationship. How could just the mention of family cause her to react so? It reminded Randall how little he really knew of Tricia, of her past.

He felt her begin to stiffen in his arms and ever so slowly begin to back away from him. "Oh, no, Princess," he whispered, tightening his hold on her. "You're not leaving me now. It's only Friday evening and we have the whole glorious weekend ahead of us."

To Randall's disappointment, only silence answered his remark. What was she thinking? He recalled that she'd spoken very little of her family, her childhood, her own life. He knew only that her mother had died and that an older aunt and uncle had adopted her. What had taught her that remoteness was the easy way out, that distance equaled safety? "We're taking Matthew fishing tomorrow," he said encouragingly, his hands slowly caressing her tense back through the silk of her dress. "Harry's going to go visit his friend, and you and I are going on a picnic. How does that sound?"

"Fine," Tricia said. She'd begun to recover from whatever emotional blow she'd been dealt. "That sounds wonderful. I guess I'm just a little tired." She smiled up at him, a tentative, apologetic smile. "Matthew snores off and on during the night, so I didn't get much rest."

"Try to sleep anyway," he said softly, relieved at her return to lightheartedness. He bent to kiss her.

On Saturday morning Harry's old friend arrived at the hotel to meet him. To Tricia's amazement Randall acted surprisingly protective of Harry. He wrote down the man's name, address, and phone number, and questioned their planned agenda as if he were sending a child off with strangers. Tricia smiled to herself. Randall was a cautious, caring person who couldn't bear to see anyone he was fond of put into a position that wasn't in their best interest.

Next they gathered rented fishing supplies and the picnic basket Tricia had ordered from the hotel's deli and set off for a day of fishing.

The fresh, cool air and bright sunshine combined to make a day perfect for fishing Tom Sawyer–style with cane poles and worms in the Mississippi River, though admittedly from a different bank than the one Tom and Huck had used.

At lunch Tricia surprised Matthew with a large illustrated book on Civil War history and a package of Confederate money she'd purchased at a gift shop. He marveled over the now-worthless currency of the defunct Confederate States of America and handled each bill and coin with an awe that confirmed Tricia's wise selection of gifts.

Not to be outdone, Randall went to the car and came back with a complete set of miniature Civil War soldiers wearing both the blue and the gray, complete with horses, cannons, and the appropriate flags.

The trio gave up their unsuccessful attempts at fishing and spent the afternoon reenacting battles, which though not historically accurate, delighted Matthew.

When at last they returned to the hotel, a message awaited Randall. Frowning, he read the message then disappeared into his room to make a phone call. Thirty minutes later Tricia answered a soft rap at her door and discovered a discouraged-looking Randall, who stepped in and looked around the room. ''Where's Matthew?''

''In the tub,'' Tricia answered apprehensively. ''What's wrong?''

''The message was from Jerry, the doctor who's answering my calls this weekend. It seems he's had a family crisis and I'm afraid that means we'll have to go back as soon as possible.''

Tricia nodded her understanding. ''Were you able to get in touch with Harry?''

''He's on his way back now.'' Randall paused. ''I hate to have to ask you to pack up now, but. . . . ''

''It's okay, Randall.'' She tried to comfort him. ''We-'ve had a lovely time. Touring the city and the antebellum homes will just have to wait for another weekend.''

''Thanks for being so understanding, Princess.'' Randall smiled and touched his hand gently to her face. Then he followed with a kiss. ''Think you can stay awake all night and talk to me while I drive?''

Tricia, who had treated herself to a nap under a giant oak tree that afternoon while the would-be generals refought the war, readily agreed. ''For you I'd go without food, water, or sleep,'' she said dramatically.

''It won't be that bad,'' he said. ''I'll let you have all the caffeine and fast food you want.''

''You've got yourself a deal, mister.''

''Do one more thing for me,'' he asked hoarsely, as if his voice was caught in his throat.

''What?''

''The holidays are coming. Spend Christmas with me. With me and Emily and Bradley,'' he asked. Then he placed a soft kiss on her lips, an action that made his invitation more appealing.

''I can't. I'm sorry. I already promised Aunt Barbara,'' she whispered. ''It's a tradition.''

''Then New Year's Eve?'' he asked. ''If you aren't going to be busy washing your hair or something.'' He mimicked the high-school boy who had heard every imaginable letdown.

''Yes,'' she said, looking up into his face, which was bent down toward her own. ''Yes,'' she repeated breathlessly. ''I will. New Year's Eve.''

Randall pulled Tricia to him and they wrapped their arms around each other to seal the promise. ''I'm sorry I disappointed you,'' he said softly.

"Disappointed me? I'm not disappointed, Randall. I'm happy. Happier than I can ever remember. This weekend made me feel like a part of something real. I'll treasure it." Tricia rose on tiptoe to punctuate her words with a kiss.

"Sweetheart," he whispered. "Will you—"

The door from the bathroom slammed shut and Matthew aproached them skipping and singing, "Randall and Tricia sittin' in a tree, K-I-S-S-I-N-G. . . . "

"All right, sport," Randall said, releasing Tricia and scooping his still-damp nephew up into his arms. "What will it take to keep you quiet about this, hmm? I don't want to have to hear that from you and your brothers every time I'm near you for the next two months."

Matthew scrunched his brow in mock concentration. "Tickle me?"

"You got it," Randall cried just before a burst of childish laughter filled the room.

Chapter Six

Tricia hoped that the harmony that had developed between her and Randall during the trip to Vicksburg would continue once they returned to Asheville, but her hopes were soon dashed on the rocks of everyday life.

After a tender good-bye kiss, Randall left Tricia and returned to the world of his office, his patients, and his practice. Tricia returned to the life she had viewed as tranquil, but that now seemed somehow empty. She waited for Randall's calls or visits, which failed to come.

As time passed, Tricia wondered if she had read too much into Randall's easy, teasing banter, or if he had been disappointed with the trip and decided not to continue their relationship. He had seemed to enjoy himself, Tricia thought, but with each day that passed without him dropping in for breakfast or even calling, she reminded herself of a lesson she'd learned while modeling in Houston—some men had high expectations after an evening out, and reacted coldly or even angrily when they were disappointed. Tricia told herself repeatedly that Randall Land wasn't that kind of man, yet his silence seemed to indicate that she'd misjudged him.

The holiday season approached, but Tricia was unable to work up any enthusiasm for yet another year of feeling like an outsider as families celebrated their joy.

Two days before Christmas Tricia packed her luggage to go to Aunt Barbara and Uncle Jim's house. The Christmas celebration at their house lasted several days. First there would be an elegant party for the faculty with whom they worked. On Christmas Eve there would be another party, smaller this time, for family and close friends. Finally Christmas Day Would be celebrated by attending church services, then Tricia and her aunt and uncle would exchange gifts and have a quiet family dinner. Never more than during the holidays did Tricia feel the weight of the tragedies she'd experienced. She wondered what Christmas memories she would have if her mother had survived the stranger's attack or if Steven had lived and they had been married as planned.

Tricia carried her suitcases to her car, then walked next door with gifts for Matthew, Mark, Micah, and Marty. Their gift to her was a thick leatherbound volume of classic fairy tales. Obviously Randall had advised them in the choice of gifts. The gesture, however, was bittersweet. It was thoughtfully chosen, but reminded her not only of the missing parts of her childhood, but also of the uncertainty of the happily-ever-after future with her own prince.

She considered calling Randall before leaving for Houston, inviting him to attend one of the parties with her, but because he had not called her or stopped by since their trip to Vicksburg, she didn't. She decided instead that she would leave a friendly note for him with Emily, to wish him happy holidays. So she penned a season's greeting to Randall, including her aunt's telephone number and address.

She sealed it in an envelope and left it in Emily's care.

Then, after walking back across the lawn between their homes, she got into her car and drove away. The barren landscape featured grass that had turned a melancholy shade of brown after a freeze and bare, leafless trees, gnarled, gray, and forlorn looking.

She thought of her Aunt Barbara's house, of the huge evergreen that would stand in the center of the den, with its festive decorations, and she was comforted.

"Patricia," Aunt Barbara cried eagerly when she arrived. "You look wonderful. Come in!"

"It's the country air," Uncle Jim agreed. "I didn't approve at first when you moved away, but it seems to have agreed with you after all. Professor Smith says that your writing improves daily. And you look healthier than ever."

"Thank you, Aunt Barbara, Uncle Jim." She sighed contentedly, sitting on a sofa in the comfortable den before the fireplace.

Before they could exchange news, their visit was interrupted by the ringing telephone. "I'll be right back," Aunt Barbara said, rising to answer it.

She returned to the room just seconds later. "Patricia, it's for you."

"For me?" she asked in surprise.

"Yes. A gentleman," she answered, her voice filled with interest. "He asked for 'Tricia.' "

Tricia walked into her uncle's study to answer her call. "Hello," she said uncertainly.

"Tricia," came Randall's voice from the other end of the line. "Why is it you left town for the holidays without even stopping to say good-bye?"

"You haven't called me since we arrived home from Mississippi three weeks ago," she answered bluntly, unable to do better under the circumstances.

"And you thought I wasn't interested in seeing you again?"

"Yes. I suppose so." *What was I supposed to think?* she wondered.

"Tricia, I'm sorry. There have been so many patients to see. I didn't mean to neglect you."

Relief flooded through her body. "Patients? That's why you haven't called?"

"Of course, Tricia. Why else? Now how long do you plan to stay away?"

"Until the twenty-sixth."

"If I can break away for a few hours, may I drive over and visit? Would your aunt and uncle mind?"

"You'd come? Oh, Randall, that would be wonderful! I'm sure they'd love to meet you."

"Okay. I'll give you a call before I come. Gotta go now. 'Tis the season to be catching the flu, you know."

"Randall?" Tricia asked curiously, "how did you know where I was? I just arrived."

"Emily," He laughed. "She brought your note over just as soon as you left."

"Emily—more dependable than the Pony Express!"

"See you soon, love."

" 'Bye, Randall." Tricia hung up the phone, still smiling. Her spirits soared, and as a drowning person grabs hold of a life preserver, she grabbed hold of the hope that she'd see him again soon.

"Who was that?" Aunt Barbara asked when Tricia returned to the room.

"Randall Land," she answered, her heart light.

"The doctor who called when you were hurt?" Uncle Jim asked.

"Yes. He may come by later if he can break away from his office."

"How lovely. Perhaps he can escort you to the faculty party tomorrow night. If this young man is special to you, then everyone should meet him."

"What makes you think he's special?"

"The sparkle in your eyes, dear. It's unmistakable. Tell us more about him."

Randall called the next day to say he'd come by in the early evening. Hospital rounds would prevent him from staying for the party, but if Tricia could dress before he arrived, then they could spend a few hours together.

When Randall arrived, Tricia answered the door.

"Wow! Let me look at you." He whistled softly when he saw her. Tricia wore a floor-length, slim dress of shining black cloth. It had elbow-length full sleeves and a sweetheart neckline. The darkness of the dress contrasted

sharply with her golden hair. When she turned, he saw
that the dress plunged sharply in the back, exposing
smooth, flawless skin. "I've never seen anything like
this!"

"It's for the party," she explained.

"Well, you've never looked lovelier."

"Come in," she said, hugging herself against the cold.

"Not yet. I have to get your gift from the car first. It
may be too cold to leave it."

"Too cold?" Tricia asked in puzzlement as Randall
walked to his car and returned with a fuzzy, whimpering
golden retriever puppy wearing a bow around its neck.

"A puppy!" she exclaimed, taking it from him and
closing the door. "He's beautiful. Thank you."

"I worry about you living alone," he said. "This little
guy will be an excellent deterrent to burglars once he's
bigger."

They sat together on the sofa. "Aunt Barbara and Uncle
Jim are upstairs dressing. They'll be down later." She
stroked the dog, who curled up on her lap. "What's his
name?"

"That's for you to decide."

"I think I'll call him Nicholas," she said with shining
eyes.

"Nicholas?"

"Yes, like Saint Nicholas, because he was a Christmas
gift."

Randall leaned near Tricia, putting his arm on the back
of the sofa around her shoulders.

"I'm glad your aunt and uncle aren't down yet. I
wanted to talk to you, about us." His voice sounded
serious.

"Us?" she asked apprehensively.

"Yes, us." Randall smiled, but there was a firmness in his manner that Tricia couldn't ignore. "Your leaving town without letting me know sent a shock wave through me. I guess I deserved it, but it was still a jolt to learn how easily I was letting you get away. I'm sorry." He sighed. "I can only guess what you've been thinking. Especially considering the circumstances."

"It doesn't matter, Randall," she interrupted, observing his worried expression. "What I thought doesn't matter anymore."

"Tricia," he whispered huskily as he bent his face toward hers. "Tricia, my dear Tricia."

He held her face between his palms, his fingers entwined in her soft hair. "How could I have been too busy for this?" he asked softly as he delivered a slow, thorough kiss.

"Randall?" Tricia asked breathlessly.

"Yes?"

"What you said a little while ago, I mean, why do you let yourself stay so busy?"

"Because I can help people," he answered simply. "When someone is hurting, I can make them feel better. When someone is ill, I can make them well again. What I can't do is walk away from them when they need me."

Tricia reflected on the sincerity of his words. She remembered how he had sat by her bedside in the hospital until she regained consciousness, how he had come during the night to check on her condition, and again the next morning. And she believed him.

"I understand," she murmured. "I just didn't want to

be in competition with something I can't possibly win out over.''

"This can't be easy for you," he said reflectively. "You deserve more, someone who can lavish time on you, pamper you.''

"It can't be easy for you, either.''

"But it's the life I've chosen. You weren't allowed the luxury of choosing.''

"Would you make the same decision now, if you had to do it over again?'' she asked earnestly.

"These people need me. I don't see what choice I have. I think of you constantly, but I don't know how to reconcile the situation.''

"Will you try? Randall, remember I need you too.''

"Yes, Princess. I promise you. I *will* find a way.''

"That sounds wonderful,'' she said, leaning against him, her head on his shoulder.

"You stay close to me, Tricia, looking the way you look tonight and telling me how you need me, and I'm liable to forget everything else, scoop you up in my arms, and carry you off to some deserted island somewhere. Or better yet, like some pirate, take you out into the middle of the ocean on a boat, where no one could ever reach us, the moonlight reflecting on the water, and the boat gently rocking with the rhythm of the ocean.''

"And then?'' she asked, her face upturned to his, her eyes shining with happiness.

"I'd kiss you like this.'' He took possession of her mouth, and his arms held her tightly.

"Patricia? Has your young man arrived?'' Uncle Jim called discreetly from the top of the stairs.

Tricia broke from Randall's embrace. "Yes, Uncle Jim. We're in the den," she called out unsteadily.

"Patricia?" Randall teased softly.

"That's what they call me," she answered quickly.

"I thought you said 'Patty Ann' was your childhood name."

"Please, Randall, I don't have time to explain now."

Uncle Jim, dressed in a tuxedo, entered the room. "Dr. Land. It's a pleasure to meet you," he said, shaking his hand.

"Professor McGill, please call me Randall."

"And you call me Jim. Would you like a drink? A holiday toast?"

"Whatever you're having."

"Patricia," Uncle Jim said jovially, noticing the furry ball on her lap. "What's that you're holding?"

"A gift from Randall," she answered, picking up the dog and holding him out for her uncle's inspection. "I'm going to call him Nicholas."

"A golden retriever, huh?" he remarked, taking the animal from her. "I approve of your choice. These are loyal animals and very protective. This is just what Patricia needs. Though she seems to be thriving, Barbara and I worry about her living alone. This dog, when it gets bigger, will be a good watchdog."

"My thoughts exactly," Randall agreed.

The men launched into a discussion of Tricia's well-being and safety, while Tricia herself poured the drinks and then reclaimed her pet from Uncle Jim.

Aunt Barbara joined the group, and before Tricia realized it was getting late, she heard the clock strike eight.

"Eight o'clock." Randall sighed. "I need to get back

to the hospital to make rounds. I've kept you from your party long enough.''

''Nonsense,'' Uncle Jim said, shaking his hand. ''It's been a real pleasure to meet you, my boy.''

''Patricia,'' Aunt Barbara said, ''Uncle Jim and I are going upstairs to get our coats. You can show Randall out and let us know when you are ready to leave for the party.''

''Thanks,'' she said, watching them disappear discreetly up the staircase.

''Nice people,'' Randall remarked. He wrapped his arms around Tricia. ''You haven't forgotten our date for New Year's Eve, have you?''

''No.'' Tricia sighed softly. ''I haven't forgotten a thing.'' She gave in once more to Randall's kisses, then, wishing him a merry Christmas, she watched him walk to his car and drive away.

''He seems like a nice young man,'' Aunt Barbara remarked approvingly as they drove toward the campus of the university for the party. ''So nice-looking, and easy to talk to.''

''Yes,'' Uncle Jim agreed. ''I liked Steven too, of course, but Randall seems more your type.''

''Randall is nice,'' Tricia agreed, but she did not give any additional information.

''Just nice?'' Aunt Barbara asked, curious about her niece's relationship with this new beau. ''He seemed more than nice.''

''He is,'' Tricia admitted, mellowing. ''He's one of those remarkable people who you can believe in. He's the kindest, most caring person I've ever known. A blend of country wit and wisdom with sophistication and intelligence.''

''Well.'' Uncle Jim laughed. ''After a visit from a man such as you have described, the old professors at this party will seem boring to you.''

''Not at all, Uncle Jim,'' Tricia countered with genuine affection. ''These people are my dear friends.''

A week passed. *New Year's Eve,* Tricia thought as she dressed for the party. *A time for new beginnings.* She remembered last New Year's Eve with an involuntary shudder. The night Steven had died. ''This year will be different,'' she told herself resolutely, fighting off a sense of unreasonable panic that threatened to overtake her as she saw Randall's car approach her house. Last New Year's Eve had marked a change in her life. Would this one?

''Happy New Year,'' she called, waving from the doorway as he came up the walk. ''come in!''

''Wow!'' he remarked, observing her dress, a sequined evening dress with thin straps over her narrow shoulders. It was by far the most daring thing she had worn in a year. ''The more I see of you, the more I like. That is one dynamite dress!''

''Thank you.'' She smiled. ''Come see Nicholas. He's growing.''

He followed her to the patio where Nicholas made his home. ''In the spring he can go outside, but he stays here for now,'' she explained.

Nicholas ran to Tricia on wobbly legs, and upon being picked up began to lick her affectionately.

''I see the two of you are getting along well.''

''Yes. He's great company.''

''What about my company?'' he asked lightheartedly.

''I wouldn't know. I never see you. A phone call now and then between patients is the most I can hope for during flu season.''

''All right, then, my New Year's resolution will be to pay more attention to you, although I'm afraid that if I take you to Houston tonight in that dress, someone may steal you away from me.''

''We're going to a party in Houston?'' she asked apprehensively. Again the wave of panic lapped at her.

''Yes. At the home of one of my friends. A man I was in medical school with. He throws a big party every year, but I rarely attend.''

''Won't that be dangerous? Driving back home, late, after the party?''

The concern in her voice, the fright in her eyes, surprised Randall. He noticed that the color had left her face. ''I tell you what,'' he volunteered, humoring her. ''I won't drink. Will that make you feel safer?''

''I'll call Aunt Barbara. We can stay there after the party, or we can get hotel rooms.''

''Tricia, nothing is going to happen.'' He tried to reason with her. ''We drove all night to get home from Vicksburg and we did just fine.''

''But on New Year's Eve there are terrible accidents on the roads.''

''Relax, sweetheart. I wouldn't do anything to endanger you.'' He paused, observing her uncertain reaction to his words. ''Go and get your coat now,'' he prompted her. ''It's cold out tonight.''

Slowly, with trembling hands, Tricia returned Nicholas to his bed. Then she went into the next room to get her coat.

"That's some coat," Randall remarked as he helped her into a thick, soft fur. "Where does a student writer get a coat like this?"

"It was a gift," she answered evasively.

"Someone has expensive taste," he remarked under his breath, annoyed at her sudden return to evasiveness, her unwillingness to answer his questions. "Shall we go?"

Small talk interspersed with short silences marked the drive to Houston, as Randall wondered about Tricia's unreasonable fear of driving home tonight, and she carefully avoided the subject by talking about other things.

Finally Randall turned his car into the streets of the elegant River Oaks section of Houston and drove slowly until he came to a stop before a large modern home.

"Your friend," Tricia said in alarm, "is Vince? Vince Johnson?"

"Yes. Do you know him?"

Tricia nodded. "From when I lived here, before I moved to Asheville. I told you I knew some doctors." She turned toward him, pale and trembling slightly. "Were you at this party last year?"

"No. I told you I rarely go to big parties," he answered, annoyed at her reluctance. "Now let's go in, shall we?"

"Yes," she said without enthusiasm, nodding her head and gathering her coat about her.

Vince Johnson, a handsome man in his mid thirties, opened the door and greeted his guest. "Randall," he cried with genuine affection. "Welcome! I'm glad you decided to come this year.'' Then, glancing to see who Randall had brought as a date, he froze momentarily.

''Patty Ann?'' he asked in amazement. ''Patty Ann McGill? What a surprise! Where have you been? How did the two of you get together? Heck, never mind all the questions! Come in. I'm sure everyone will want to see you.'' Vince leaned forward, took Tricia's hand, and kissed her face as he pulled her farther into the room.

Still holding her hand, he called to a tall, willowly redhead nearby. ''Lorrie, Lorrie! Look who's here. Patty Ann.''

The statuesque woman walked to where they stood and, with squeals of delight, led Tricia away to show her to the other guests. With many backward glances, Tricia followed.

''Well, Randall,'' Vince said, ''you certainly captured the grand prize. Where did you find Patty Ann?''

''Tricia moved to Asheville early last spring. She lives next door to my sister Emily,'' he answered, noting that everyone here called Tricia ''Patty Ann,'' the name she had given him when she was barely conscious in the hospital, then had explained away as a childhood name.

''Tricia?'' Vince asked quizzically. ''Oh, yes. That's right. I saw her uncle at a dinner party several months ago, and he told me she didn't want to be called Patty Ann anymore. He and Barbara call her 'Patricia' now—a compromise.''

''I noticed that they called her Patricia when I visited.''

''So,'' Vince remarked, ''you've met the folks. Does this mean it's serious between you and the lady? Is there something we should know?''

"I don't know that there's any big announcement pending." Randall answered noncommittally, keeping careful watch of Tricia's movements across the room. "But there is that possibility."

"Drink?" Vince asked.

"No thanks, Vince. I promised Tricia I wouldn't drink tonight. For some reason she seemed terribly frightened when I told her we were driving to Houston tonight for this party."

"Small wonder," Vince remarked. "I'm surprised you were even able to get her into a car tonight after what happened last year."

"What happened last year, Vince?" Randall asked meaningfully.

"You don't know?" he asked in disbelief. "She didn't tell you?" Vince glanced around the crowded room. "Follow me, Randall. We need to talk."

"But what about Tricia?" he protested.

"She'll be just fine. She knows almost everyone here."

Vince led his old friend into his study and closed and locked the door.

From across the room, Tricia watched suspiciously as the door to the study closed on Vince and Randall. No, *Vince,* she thought. *Don't tell him. Don't do that to me.*

"Patty Ann." A mellow male voice came from behind her as she stared at the closed door. "You look beautiful. You've never looked better."

Tricia turned to spy one of the owners of the modeling agency she had worked for, a gentleman of about fifty, with gray-speckled hair and bright, keen eyes.

"Hello, Dale. Thank you," she said graciously.

"Have a drink," he said, handing her a tall, frosty glass. "The excitement has caused you to pale. This may add some color to your cheeks."

"Thanks," she said, taking the glass. "You always knew just what I needed."

"Are you here alone?"

"No. Vince took my date away," she said, trying to sound casual. "It seems they're old friends from school. I hope he comes back soon, though. I'm afraid I feel rather nervous tonight; I could use someone to lean on."

"That's understandable," he smiled sympathetically. "I don't suppose I could be so lucky that you're ready to come back to work?"

"No, Dale. I'm through with that life. I'm studying writing."

"Writing? Don't tell me that column you used to do for the magazine has gone to your head."

"No, Dale, not at all. The editors of that magazine asked me to do a monthly column on beauty and fashion tips for their readers, but the truth is nothing I wrote ever made it into print. Oh, the ideas were mine, but never the words. I suppose I wrote so poorly that they had to hire a ghost writer to make the articles printable."

"I didn't know."

"It's not one of those things I brag about," she answered with self-deprecation.

"You were never a braggart, Patty Ann. That's what made you so easy to work with. You never reminded the other girls that you were our most requested model."

"Or that I never really finished high school," she countered.

"Or that you made a fortune for the agency," he reminded her with a smile. "What is this? I feel as if I'm playing chess. You'll never get checkmate, Patty Ann. I have something good to say about you for every negative thing you can say about yourself. And if you're studying to be a writer, Patty Ann, I'm sure you'll be a very good one."

"Tricia?" came Randall's voice from behind her. "I'm sorry Vince kept me so long. We had a lot of catching up to do."

"Oh, Randall." Tricia sighed with relief, putting her hand on his arm. "Meet Dale. I used to work for him."

"So this is the brave man who felt confident enough to leave you alone in this group," Dale said socially, extending his hand to Randall. "Thank you for bringing her here tonight. It's done me good to see her again." He turned to Tricia. "Remember, if you ever decide to come back to work, all it takes is a phone call. There's always an opening for you."

"Not a chance, Dale, but thanks."

Dale kissed Tricia and walked away.

"He seemed nice," Randall observed.

"Yes, he was," Tricia stated simply. "A good man to work for, fair and even-tempered."

Randall handed Tricia a drink. "I brought you some soda."

"Thank you, Randall," she said, glancing around the crowded room.

"It seems that we have some mutual friends. Vince, for example."

"Yes," she answered nervously. "When you asked me to a party, I never guessed it would be Vince's."

"We were interns together at the hospital. No one ever quite forgets those days, I think."

"Tell me about them," Tricia said, sipping from her glass, desperately trying to avoid the obvious topic of conversation after his talk with Vince.

Throughout the evening they were continually interrupted by his friends or her friends, someone who hadn't seen one or the other of them for quite some time and wanted to talk. Part of the evening they were together; part of the evening they were apart. But always their eyes sought each other in the crowd. Randall kept a watchful eye on Tricia, concerned about her, especially after learning the facts Vince had shared. Tricia's eyes continually sought out Randall, like a tightrope walker who stares at a fixed spot in order to maintain balance.

It seemed that every time some old friend hustled Randall away, men approached Tricia, talking to her, inquiring if she was back in town. The crowd and her own nervousness had made Tricia feel warm, and without at first realizing it she began to feel a little faint.

"The men here certainly find you intriguing tonight, Patty Ann, dear," Vince said, finding her alone for a moment late in the evening. "It must be that dress," he said, appraising her openly.

Tricia smiled unsteadily and waved away the drink he offered her. "I don't drink."

"What's the story with Randall Land? Are the two of you serious about each other?"

"Randall," Tricia mused, feeling slightly lightheaded from the throngs of people in the room. "Randall is as wonderful as he is busy."

"Too busy for you, Patty Ann? The man is a fool.

I've always told you that I'd drop anything I was doing, anytime, to be with you,'' he remarked.

"Vince.'' She blushed, "Please stop. I've forgotten what it's like to have men . . . what's that expression you use?''

"Hitting on you?'' he suggested.

"Yes. I've forgotten how to play the game, how to react.''

"You're very appealing when you blush like that. So innocent and naive,'' he said, putting his arm around her in a brotherly fashion. "There's not much innocence or naïveté to be found in this house tonight. I suppose my male guests have been hitting on you all evening?''

"You've invited a great many single men.''

"Most of them you've met before. Like Jack, over there in the blue chair.'' He gestured across the room to an attractive man who was smiling broadly at the woman standing beside him.

"Lorrie used to say Jack never married because he could never be satisfied with just one woman.''

Vince smiled. "You remember all the old gossip.'' He paused, a melancholy pause. "We miss you, dear. Do you miss us?''

"Oh, Vince. I just had to go. Everything was closing in on me. Life seemed so . . . so . . . like there wasn't any future.'' Vince had always been easy to talk to.

"And now?''

"Now? Vince.'' Her voice suddenly became alarmed, and her hand reached out to his arm for support. "I can't think clearly. Vince, I don't feel well.'' Her skin felt suddenly cold and clammy, and she swayed unsteadily on her feet.

Vince appraised her with practiced eyes. "You don't look well, either. You're pale and sweaty. What's making you feel this way?"

"I don't know. I guess I was nervous about coming here tonight."

"I'll get Randall for you."

"No," she cried softly but insistently. "No, please. Just take me to a bathroom where I can freshen up."

"All right, my dear," he said, leading her up the staircase, talking to her as if to a child. "I'll help you, and everything will be just fine. Have you eaten anything?"

"No. Not since lunch."

"Then while you freshen up, I'll get you some food. That will help."

They reached the bathroom, which was located off Vince's bedroom, and he helped her inside and closed the door. She leaned against the vanity as he ran cool water over a cloth and began to wipe her smooth skin, her shoulders, neck, and arms.

"Oh, that feels so wonderful, Vince," Tricia murmured, closing her eyes and involuntarily clinging to him for support.

"Yes? Well, if it feels that good, then perhaps you'd better do it yourself while I go get you a plate of food. Randall's an old friend, and I wouldn't want anyone to see us together like this."

"What do you mean, Vince?" she asked, not able to comprehend the sudden cooling of his attitude toward her.

"We're alone, the two of us, in my bedroom. People will most certainly talk."

"Why would they?" she asked innocently.

"Don't you know?" He paused uncertainly. "I've always been crazy about you, Patty Ann. If I believed in love, I'd say I've been in love with you for years."

Tricia looked at him in wide-eyed astonishment. "You? Then why?"

"Why? Why do I play the big brother role? It's simple. I like you too much to hurt you. If you and I were to marry, for instance, I'd adore you—at first. Your innocence would delight me, but after living with me for a while you'd wise up. Then we'd settle down to a humdrum existence, or worse, grow to despise each other. No, I like you too much to be the one to disillusion you."

"But . . . but . . ." she stuttered in confusion.

"No comment necessary, my dear," he muttered smoothly.

"Must love be a disillusionment?" Tricia asked, trusting Vince for a truthful answer.

He stared at her intently for a moment. "No, my dear. Not for the right man and the right woman. Unfortunately I'm just not the right man. I know myself well enough to admit that." He handed her the cool washcloth and walked briskly from the room.

Tricia stood alone in the bathroom, pressing the cool cloth to her skin as she waited for Vince to return. Then, with a shock, she became aware of her own mocking reflection in the mirror: the artfully applied makeup; the expensive, suggestive dress; her hair put up in a smooth, sleek style, exposing her slender neck and narrow shoulders. "Patty Ann," she gasped in horror. "Go away, Patty Ann," she said menacingly to the visage that peered back at her from the glass. "I want Tricia back."

A soft tap at the door startled her. Then the door opened and Randall, not Vince, stepped inside with a plate of hors d'oeuvres. "Vince told me you weren't feeling well," he said calmly. "Eat this, then we're going back down to join the others."

"Do we have to?" she muttered. "I'm really not feeling very social."

"It's almost midnight, Tricia. And I don't think it's healthy for you to be up here alone, talking to yourself." He handed her the plate, which she set on the vanity.

"You heard me?" she asked, noting the quiet emphasis he'd placed on the word *healthy*.

"Yes. I heard you."

After a few minutes of silence she muttered, "I'm fine now, Randall. I just needed a few minutes to get myself together."

"Eat. Then let's go downstairs with the rest of the guests. We'll leave after the New Year's toast."

"You're angry with me, aren't you?"

"No, Tricia, I could never be angry with you. I'm just a bit overwhelmed."

Chapter Seven

Alittle after midnight Randall led Tricia through the frosty air from Vince's house to his car. He opened the door for her and she slid into her seat, buckled her safety belt, and closed her eyes for a moment, wishing she could be alone. Randall shut the door, then went around to his own side and started the car.

"Tricia?"

"Yes, Randall," she said, opening her eyes.

"Are you all right?" he asked meaningfully.

"I don't know. My head feels strange."

"Did I make a fool of myself?" she asked miserably.

"No. Not at all, though some people, and I am one of them, were concerned." He paused thoughtfully before continuing. "I had no idea this evening would be so traumatic for you. The same day of the year, the same people, the same party. Believe me, Tricia. I didn't

107

know. I would never have put you through this if I had known.''

"I do believe you,'' she answered wearily. "But as for the others, if they acted concerned, it was for their own benefit, or maybe for yours, but not mine.''

"Tricia, it's unlike you to be so cynical. They're your friends. They care about you.''

"Care about me? Don't you find it odd that those people who claim to care so much about me haven't called or come to visit me in almost a year? They can't have been too worried about how I was. The last time I saw most of them was at the funeral.''

"They all expressed concern tonight. You were the one who moved away, Tricia. Maybe you made it too hard for them to locate you.''

"Too hard? A call to my aunt and uncle would have solved the mystery of my whereabouts. Or they could have gone to the post office for my forwarding address. There are many ways they could have found me, if they really had wanted to.''

"Why don't you give them a break? You make them sound so shallow. Some of them are my friends too, and I know them to be caring people.''

"Do we have to have this discussion right now?''

"Why not now?''

"Because I would feel more comfortable if you gave the driving one hundred percent of your attention now.''

"Tricia,'' he said softly. "Last year your fiancé was killed in an auto accident while driving home from Vince's party. That does not mean—''

"Are you wearing a seat belt?'' she interrupted.

"Yes, Tricia, I am. Now, what I was trying to say—''

"You can say it just as well when we get back to my house."

The rest of the drive home was silent. Randall watched both the road and Tricia, who seemed absorbed in her own thoughts. She sat silently, staring out of the window, her face turned away from him.

They arrived safely at Tricia's house between one and two in the morning and went inside. Tricia walked through the darkness into the living area and sat in a chair without turning on any lights. Randall reached for a lamp, turned it on, and then sat in a chair across from her. Under his steady gaze Tricia remained silent for several minutes before she spoke again.

"I didn't intend for you to learn the truth about me. I had hoped you'd never know."

"Why not?"

"Because you might not understand the things I've done. You might have a different opinion of me, or something like that. I wanted to leave it all, leave them all behind." Tricia was ill-prepared for the conversation, and she felt as if she lacked adequate words for an explanation. She regretted going to the party. More than that, she regretted not being able to phrase her words accurately because it seemed so important to do so.

They sat silently for a moment, then Randall spoke. "Tell me what you're thinking."

"I was thinking of how I detest some of those people at the party tonight, wondering how I ever could have been one of them. How foolish I was, how shallow."

"What are you talking about, Tricia?"

Tricia struggled for a way to explain her dilemma

clearly to him. "Suppose you gave someone a gift, a Christmas gift. Let's say the person was a child, or maybe someone from another culture, someone not familiar with our traditions. You spent time picking out the perfect gift, then you had it wrapped. But when you gave the gift to the person they thought the wrapping was so beautiful that they didn't need to open the gift. The outer wrapping was enough for them; they didn't want to go any further. They were satisfied. But you wanted them to open it. A great deal of thought had gone into choosing the gift, and you wanted them to see it and enjoy it, to appreciate the present you'd given."

"What does that analogy have to do with you?"

"I was the gift. Can't you see that? All anyone cared about was the outside, what I looked like. No one cared enough to open the gift and see what was there. No one wanted to get to know me on the inside, the real me. The outer wrapping was enough for them. But it wasn't enough for me."

"And so you left them all behind and moved to Asheville to start all over."

"Yes." She sighed, pleased that he understood. "Exactly."

Then he rose, walked to her bar, and poured himself a glass of water. "You ran away from your past, Tricia, or Patty Ann, or whoever you are," he said sternly.

"I did not run away. I made a change, a fresh start."

"Is being admired for your beauty so bad that you had to change everything?"

She sat silently and did not reply, and so he continued.

"It just seems odd to me. You didn't just move. You

changed your whole life: your job, your friends, even your name. That all seems rather drastic."

"I thought you would understand," she said glumly.

"A person doesn't just turn her back on her whole life because people admire her beauty. Why didn't you give them time to know you?"

"It's not that simple."

"Why not?"

"It's so complicated. Didn't Vince tell you, when the two of you talked at the party?"

"He told me many things," Randall said, returning to his seat across from hers. "Many surprising things about you, but nothing terrible. Nothing that would cause you to exile yourself."

Tricia took a deep breath. "I killed two people," she said with overstated simplicity. She then studied Randall to observe his reaction.

"You did what?"

"I killed two people, Dr. Steven Carey and Bubba Andrews."

"They died in an accident. You weren't responsible for the accident."

"Yes, I am."

"How?"

"The night of the accident . . ." she began, but then her strained voice trailed away, leaving the story untold.

Randall realized they were close to a breakthrough.

"Why don't you start at the beginning?" he asked.

"The beginning? Which beginning?" she asked in confusion.

"Okay then, just tell me what happened the night they died."

"There was a party, a big New Year's Eve party, like tonight. Steven and I were invited. Among the guests were people from the hospital where Vince and Steven worked, some of the same people who were there tonight." Tricia spoke very slowly, as if she were reliving each moment as it had happened. "There were other people there too. Anyway, Steven and I had been secretly engaged for several months. We didn't want to tell anyone because Steven was so much older than I was. We felt that some people would be critical. So we made plans to marry quietly in the spring. That way the deed would be done, and maybe once people saw that we were content, they wouldn't be so critical."

Randall wanted to ask her why she had used the word "content" rather than "happy," but she continued.

"Bubba was at the party also. I guess you could say he was infatuated with me. He followed me around. He wanted me to leave the party with him. He had been calling me for more than a year, trying to get me to go out with him. But that night he'd been drinking heavily, and he wasn't easily discouraged. He wouldn't be reasonable. I tried to put him off, ignore him, but he persisted. He said that all he wanted was for me to go out with him; he said that was all he'd ever wanted."

"Why didn't you? Bubba was a well-known athlete. Most women would have been flattered by his attention."

She looked at him with something akin to disgust in her eyes. "Would you want to go out with someone twice your size and half your IQ?"

"Good point." He smiled.

"Anyway, Steven noticed Bubba bothering me. After

midnight he called for everyone's attention. He announced our engagement. We had agreed not to, but he thought it would stop Bubba?''

"Did it stop Bubba?''

"No. Bubba became angry and made a terrible scene, threatening Steven, calling me terrible things, saying that Steven had bought me and that I couldn't handle a real man. Steven and I left the party and went back to my apartment. The police theorize that Bubba followed us. Steven came in for a short time, then he left. Bubba was outside, waiting. He followed Steven. The theory is that Bubba tried to run Steven off the road. Somehow they collided. They both died in the fiery crash.'' She remained silent for a long moment as tears made their way down her smooth face. "They burned to death,'' she said solemnly, wiping the tears with the back of her hand. "It's just too horrible to think about.''

"Horrible, yes. But not your fault.''

"How can you sit there so calmly and not be shocked and angry over all you've learned about me tonight?''

"I already knew who you are, or were, before tonight,'' Randall said matter-of-factly. "I didn't know everything, but I knew.''

"How?'' she asked, her eyes widening. "I didn't tell anyone.''

"Early in our relationship you mentioned that you were a writer. While I was in the library one day I decided to look in the *Reader's Guide* to see what type of articles you'd written. To my surprise, I found articles *about* you, not by you. It was 'Patricia McGill,' of course, not 'Tricia,' but you had told me Tricia was a nickname. A quick glance at the titles gave me the answers to some of the things I'd been wondering about.''

''I guess I haven't hidden my past as well as I thought I had.''

''It doesn't matter, Tricia. You are the only one bothered by your past. No one else thinks you are responsible for those deaths. Can't you see? You're the victim, not the criminal.''

''You don't think I'm responsible for their horrible deaths?''

''No. But I do think you're confused.''

''You do?''

''Yes. And I love you, Tricia. I don't want to see you hurt like this.''

''Even now? Now that you know?''

''Nothing to know. Nothing to diminish my love. You tried to run away from an unpleasant memory. People have done worse,'' he said philosophically. ''Though I think you'd be happier if you'd face the truth as the truth. It happened. It's over. That's all. You must get on with your life.''

''My life?''

''Our lives, Tricia,'' he said tenderly. ''Hopefully, our lives together.''

''Will you hold me?''

''Of course, dear.'' He took her into his arms, and she clung to him, holding on as if she feared drowning in a sea of bad memories and a rushing tide of swirling emotions.

He held her for a long moment, feeling her slump tiredly in his arms. ''You've had a long, traumatic evening. Now go upstairs and go to bed.'' He turned her toward the stairs and gave her a small push. "Go on now."

Tricia obeyed, too tired to protest.

"My head hurts, Randall."

"It will feel better in the morning. Now, please go to bed."

Tricia began to walk slowly up the dark stairs. Halfway she stopped briefly and looked back before proceeding.

Randall watched her until she disappeared into her room.

"I love you," he whispered into the darkness.

Chapter Eight

Probably because of the unsettling conversation she'd had with Randall, Tricia slept little that night. When she did sleep, her dreams were troubled, and more the once Tricia traveled to the scene of the fiery auto accident that had taken the life of her fiancé.

She finally awoke early. From her window she could see the heavy gray sky, which gave no hint of coming sunshine. Because it seemed a chill had settled on the world, Tricia pulled on a thick, warm robe and started downstairs.

Halfway down the stairs Tricia noted, with great surprise, that Randall was asleep on the sofa. His tie, jacket, and shoes had been removed and his shirt collar loosened, but otherwise he was still dressed. His hair was uncombed, and he looked more vulnerable than she had ever seen him, almost like a little boy. Tricia wondered vaguely why he had stayed.

Quietly she went into the kitchen and began to make coffee. While it brewed she brought Nicholas his food and stroked him, crooning softly to him until the coffee was ready. "How could I have been such a fool?" she asked. But Nicholas only looked at her with wide brown eyes as if to say "I don't understand it, either."

She poured the steaming coffee into two cups and brought them in to Randall, who was now beginning to awaken.

She handed him a mug filled with coffee, then sat and wrapped both her hands around her own mug as if it were the only warmth in her life.

"Good morning, Randall," she said softly.

"Morning, Tricia," he said wearily, sitting up to drink his coffee and running his fingers through his uncombed hair. "How do you feel this morning?"

"I don't know. Numb, I guess." She spoke in a dull, emotionless tone.

"Do you feel up to talking about it?" he asked.

"What would you like to know?" she asked in a tone of weary resignation. She owed him at least that much. She'd answer his questions and hope, only hope, that he could forgive her.

"Everything. Why did you come here? Was it a conscious decision, an effort to bury the past? Or was it an impulse, a hasty action that you started and then were too proud to go back on?"

"It was deliberate," she answered. "I remember the exact day I realized just how much I hated my modeling job. I was in New York doing live modeling. Not pictures, but modeling clothes for buyers. The manufacturers had coached me on what to say. There I was, wearing this ridiculously expensive dress and saying, 'It's important to remember that when you buy, you're not buying just a dress. You're purchasing a fashion statement.' Repeating what they'd told me to say, like a parrot! It sounded so ridiculous. I was disgusted with myself.

"Then, that same evening, after a turbulent flight back to Houston, my agent showed up at my apartment with an offer from one of those horrible magazines, you know the kind. They wanted to pay me to do a nude centerfold. He said he thought it would be a great career move. Can you believe that? I was so furious I tore up my contract, fired my agent. That was the end of my modeling career. I couldn't stand it. It made me feel dirty." Tricia shivered involuntarily. "I don't know how Mother could stand it all those years," she said to herself.

"Your mother was a model also?"

Tricia swallowed, then answered. "Yes," she said lifelessly. "And she didn't die in an accident as I told you. She was murdered." Tricia looked at Randall to see if the news had shocked him.

"Did the police discover who killed her?" he asked.

"No." She paused. "Aunt Barbara said they kept it quiet to protect me. You see, I was in the next room. I heard her scream, I listened to her struggle, but I was so terrified that I didn't do anything. I didn't go for help. I heard the man run from the apartment, but I didn't see him, so I couldn't identify him. I should have done something. Then I could have told the authorities, and maybe he would have been made to pay for what he'd done. Instead, I hid under my bed. He didn't know I was there, or he probably would have killed me too. The police told Aunt Barbara and Uncle Jim that if the man who killed Mother found out that I was there, he might come after me, thinking that I had seen something. So the police kept it as quiet as possible. Aunt Barbara and Uncle Jim took me away. When we left the apartment, we closed the door on that part of my life. They adopted me, gave me their last name. My early life was rarely mentioned, as if it never happened.''

"So you learned early that you could just walk away from your life if it was painful. Close the door and leave. Start over again. Bury the pain. And you learned something else, equally dangerous. You learned to blame yourself for things that were not within your power to control.''

"There must be something wrong with me if I let these things happen. I allow bad things to happen to the people I love.''

"How could you have stopped them?''

"Mother—I heard it all. I could have called the police or run to the neighbors for help.''

"That man would have caught you and killed you before you succeeded. You were five years old, Tricia. A baby!''

"And Steven," she continued as if she had not heard him. "I could have stopped Bubba.''

"How, Tricia? You didn't know what he was planning to do. He was drunk, jealous, and angry that you had chosen Steven over him. He probably didn't even know what he was doing. ''The bad things that have happened in your past—none of them were your fault. Let go. Quit blaming yourself for them. Concentrate on the good things; the things you are responsible for. Tricia, having been a top model is not something to be ashamed of. Many girls dream of achieving what you did.''

''You don't understand. I never worked for that success or planned on it. I didn't do anything to deserve it. Beauty is inherited, not earned. Clothes can be bought. Believe me, modeling is a shallow, meaningless life— all appearance and no depth.''

''Then why did you do it?''

''I never had any intention of getting involved in modeling. It kind of just happened, like everything else in my life up to this point. A friend of mine from school entered the Miss Houston pageant. She convinced me to enter with her. I didn't see any reason not to, and I thought I might have an outside chance of winning one of the talent scholarships they give. I never even thought I'd win, never gave any consideration to how my life would be affected if I did win. I was a runner-up, but what is more important is that one of the judges was Dale, the man you met at Vince's party. He approached me and asked me to join the agency. I think he mistook indifference for poise,'' she said self-deprecatingly.

''I was still in high school when all of this happened, far too young. Anyway, against my aunt and uncle's wishes, he arranged for me to quit school and get a Graduate Equivalency Degree. So while the other kids went to the prom and graduation parties, I was modeling, earning more than most of them ever would and living on my own. I wasn't learning and doing normal teenage things. I felt comfortable talking to reporters and posing for cameras, but awkward with normal teenage things. Instead of learning to date nice young men, I learned the tricks of fighting off overly amorous men. I felt so different.'' She looked at him sadly. ''I just didn't fit in.''

Randall looked at her sympathetically. ''Go on,'' he encouraged.

''I made friends with other models, mostly older, more experienced, worldly girls. They enjoyed bringing me to parties and introducing me to men. Generally speaking, the men at those parties took an interest in models only for reasons you can easily surmise.''

''And Dr. Carey?''

''Strangely enough, I met him at one of those parties.'' She paused, as if remembering, then continued. ''It was a crowded, noisy party at someone's house. It was a big, beautiful home, but I don't remember whose it was. The room was stuffy and heavy with smoke, so I stepped out onto the balcony, into the darkness of the night. The air smelled fresh. There was the fragrance of flowers in bloom in the garden. The skies were clear, and it was quiet. I leaned against the railing, looking up at the stars, and thought how I preferred the solitude of the dark to the sounds and sights and smells of the party. Suddenly someone spoke. I turned, startled, to see Steven. I hadn't realized he was there, sitting in a chair, sipping a drink, enjoying his own solitude until I had invaded it. He politely asked me to join him, and, as that seemed preferable to returning to the party, I did.

''I learned that Steven's wife had died a few months before. As he spoke of his loneliness, I somehow felt close to him. He wasn't threatening. He was a mild, gentle man. We sat on the balcony for several hours, making small talk. He didn't make any advances toward me or ask if he could call. Steven was much older than me.''

"Yes. Dr. Carey was the chief of surgery when I was an intern. He must have been in his fifties."

"I didn't see him again, didn't think about it. A few months later Aunt Barbara had to be hospitalized for a few days. I went to the hospital as much as possible to be with her. Steven saw me in the hallway at noon one day. He recognized me and asked me to have lunch with him. The lunch went well. He asked me out. We began going places together: the theater, sporting events, out to eat. He was easy to talk to, easy to get to know. I felt comfortable with him."

"Tricia, was *comfortable* enough for you to agree to marry him? Weren't you in love with him?"

"No." She shook her head sadly. "I wasn't in love with him. Maybe I thought I'd grow to love him after we were married. I don't know, but I had never been in love. I wasn't sure it really existed. Much later I realized that Steven wanted me only as a companion." Her voice grew speculative. "He must have still loved his wife very much."

"And what did other people say? Your families?"

"About the marriage?"

He nodded.

"Aunt Barbara and Uncle Jim questioned it at first, but they didn't object. They always seemed to be just a little awed by the events of my life, and so I guess they felt relieved I was going to settle down with someone respectable and secure."

"And his family?"

"His children were vehemently against the marriage. They argued that I was too young for him. When he died they blamed me."

"How do you know?"

"They made horrible accusations against me both privately and publicly. I can't begin to tell you. They even spoke to an attorney to see if I could be held legally responsible for his death. They talked of filing a suit against me, claiming I led Bubba on and was responsible for the results of what happened."

"They were wrong, Tricia."

She looked at him for an expressionless moment. Finally she continued her story. "Steven left me some money in his will. With that money and my savings from modeling, I moved here."

"And once again closed a door on part of your life. Until last night."

"Yes." She shrugged her shoulders. "Until last night."

There was an awkward silence between them. Finally she spoke. "Why did you stay?"

"I thought you might need me, Tricia, but you didn't. I hoped you might call out to me in the night, or come down those stairs and say that you'd made a mistake, that it was me you needed, not Steven or Bubba. But it didn't happen. You didn't need me. You're a remarkably strong woman in some ways, Tricia."

"Are you angry about last night at the party? I wasn't really prepared to see all those people."

"Tricia, I need time to sort this all out. I think you do too. Things are much more complicated than I thought, and rushing into another relationship could make things worse for you."

"You said you loved me."

"I do, Tricia, but sometimes love just isn't the answer to all the questions. Sometimes life isn't that simple."

"You're punishing me for the things I did last night."

"No, Tricia." He sighed wearily. "I'm not punishing you. There's more to you than that. There's more to me than that. A mutual loving relationship, one that works, is the hardest thing in the world to find." His eyes searched Tricia's face as he spoke, as if seeking to find the answers to his questions there. "I wish I knew how to help you."

"You think I'm crazy?"

"No. Of course not. The world is crazy. Considering all you've been through, you're a miracle. You're surviving the best way you know how. Doing what you've learned to do. Your mother died, and you had to start all over, begin a new life. When you left high school to model, your life changed and you found you were different from your school friends, so you closed a door on that part of your life, made new friends, and started over. Then Steven died and you tried to block out that part of your life too. You learned to survive by changing, adapting, forgetting the past. But last night you found out that you can't do that anymore."

"Tell me what to do," she pleaded.

"You'll have to decide that for yourself, dear." He rose and began to gather his things.

"You're leaving?"

"Yes, Tricia. We both need time. Time alone, to make important decisions. I think it would be better if we didn't see each other for a while." He reached out, touched her face, and turned to go.

"Don't leave me, Randall. Don't you leave me too," she cried out piteously as he closed the door.

A new year, Tricia thought disgustedly to herself. *A new year for new mistakes.* She curled her body into a ball and cried into a pillow. She cried for the father she never knew, for the mother she had loved, then been denied. She cried for her friends at school, the people she had given up on too soon. She cried for Steven. And finally, she cried for herself, tears of self-pity, something she had never in all her life allowed herself to do.

A few days later Matthew appeared at Tricia's door bundled in a coat and a hat and holding a small, thin tree limb with a diaper tied to it flag-style.

"We surrender," he said with an exaggerated salute when Tricia opened her door and looked down at him in surprise.

"What?"

"Uncle Randall is baby-sittin' us while Mommy and Daddy are gone somewhere. He said for me to come over and say 'we surrender.' "

"Tell him—" Tricia began.

"Tell him what?" a masculine voice asked, and Tricia looked into Randall's smiling face. Marty was perched on his shoulders. Micah and Mark stood close by his side.

"We wanna play with Nicholas," Micah proclaimed.

"He's on the patio. You know where it is," she said as the boys rushed past her, shedding coats, hats, and gloves as they ran. "What's this about a surrender?" she asked Randall after the boys were out of hearing. "Conditional or unconditional?"

"I was thinking of something more in the way of a truce," he said, smiling and leaning his shoulder casually against the wall in her entryway.

"Truce accepted," she said, putting her hand forward.

"No handshakes," he said, leaning toward her, taking Marty from his shoulders and settling him on the floor. "We'll seal this one with a kiss."

"Uncle Randall, quit kissin' and come see what Nicholas can do!" Matthew interrupted, pulling on Randall's shirt. "Uncle Randall!"

"Duty calls," Randall whispered, breaking from Tricia's tender embrace.

"I'll come with you. I have hot chocolate and cookies for the boys and some dog biscuits for Nicholas. Where are Emily and Bradley?" Tricia asked curiously.

"They've taken the day off to celebrate."

"Celebrate?"

"Yes, Emily is pregnant. Again."

"Oh, Randall—five!" Tricia gasped, observing the four robust boys fighting for Nicholas's attention. "How wonderful!" she paused, smiling. "How late will they be out?"

"Till about eight."

"I could cook dinner, Randall, to celebrate our truce," Tricia offered with a gleam in her blue eyes.

"Sorry, Princess, when they return I'll have to dash over to the hospital to check on a few patients." Randall observed Tricia's face, her obvious disappointment. "How about tomorrow night? There are a few things I have to take care of, but I'll try to do those early. I can get here about seven."

"Seven would be wonderful." She sighed happily. "Any time with you would be wonderful."

Randall smiled as he turned his car into Tricia's driveway. He thought of the flowers he had sent her earlier that day, and he felt inside the breast pocket of his coat. The ring was there. There was no doubt in his mind that he loved Tricia. True, there were still some ghosts from her past haunting her, but he was determined he could chase them away, and tonight would be the night. After tonight there would be no room in Tricia's mind or heart for anyone else. What she needed was reassurance of constant love, and he could best provide that within the framework of marriage. Also true was the fact that his practice demanded an overwhelming amount of his time, but he believed marriage would help that too. At least he could come home to Tricia each night, even if it was late. He turned off the car's engine, picked up the bottle of wine he had chosen for tonight's dinner, and hummed to himself as he walked toward Tricia's door.

"Hi, Randall," Tricia greeted him, opening the door even before he rang the bell. "Come on in."

Randall thought he could detect slight annoyance in her voice as he entered and closed the door. "Is that the warmest greeting I get?" he teased innocently, determined to get the evening off to a good start. "How about a kiss?"

Tricia paused for a moment, then smiled. "I'm sorry, Randall. Of course I'm glad to see you." She lifted her arms to embrace him, and his arms encircled her.

"Now, what's the problem?" he asked consolingly as he kissed her forehead, eyelids, nose, and lips.

"You're late," she said without recrimination, looking into his handsome, honest face. "And I guess I got frustrated trying to keep dinner warm. I wanted everything to be perfect tonight."

"I'm here now," Randall answered, pulling her close to him. "And tonight will be memorable."

Tricia led Randall into the dining room, where the table was set, complete with candles and the fresh flowers he had sent.

"It's lovely," he complimented Tricia. "Almost as lovely as you are."

"Pour the wine, and I'll serve dinner," she suggested. "I hope you like it. It's a seafood casserole Aunt Barbara makes on special occasions."

"I could get used to this." Randall sighed, enjoying the leisurely dinner, the candlelight, and the company.

Tricia smiled. "I hope so. I hope there will be many evenings like this one."

After they had eaten, Randall rose, took Tricia's hand, and led her into the living area. He took off his jacket and carefully laid it on a nearby end table, aware of the treasure that rested in the pocket. Then they sat together on a sofa in the dim light. Tricia arranged herself comfortably against Randall, fitting snugly against him.

Randall thought for a moment that he'd call a travel agent and wisk Tricia off to one of those old castles in Europe for their honeymoon. In Randall's thoughts Europe was definitely the place. A castle with heavy beamed ceilings and huge fireplaces, where generations of kings romanced their queens.

"What's wrong, Tricia?" he asked softly, "You seem so reserved tonight."

"Why were you late? Patients again?" Tricia asked gently, positioning herself to look into his eyes.

"Yes, Tricia," he said, his eyes meeting hers. "My responsibility to them is the only thing that could ever keep me from getting here. It's a hazard of the profession I've learned to accept."

Tricia smiled. "Then I'll learn to accept it too." Her hands went to the outline of Randall's face, framing it and holding it captive, and her lips went to meet his in a thoughtful manner.

Randall pulled her closer. For endless moments they held one another. Then, suddenly, Tricia broke away. Tricia realized how rapidly her heart was beating.

Randall looked at her in astonishment.

"Randall," Tricia said, reaching out to soothingly. "I'm sorry. I've had an awfully frustrating day. I still have work to do, and I feel very tense and distracted."

Randall looked at her thoughtfully for a moment. "What's really bothering you, Princess?"

"Do you remember the story I was writing?"

He nodded.

"I just can't get the rewrites done. I've tried all day, but everything I write sounds flat and unfeeling. If I don't finish soon, the publisher may withdraw his offer."

"What's giving you trouble?" Randall asked.

Tricia stared at him wide-eyed, feeling slightly embarrassed. "He wants the love scenes rewritten."

Randall laughed. "Is that it. I read the story. Well, those scenes *were* a little lifeless."

Tricia bristled. "You don't have to laugh," she said icily.

Randall remembered hearing that artists were sensitive

about criticism of their work, and he tried to repair any damage he may have made. "It's an excellent story, Tricia. The characters are well drawn and complex. Don't worry so much. I'll help you, if you want." He winked at her.

"Don't be condescending, Randall," she retorted coolly. "I don't tell you how to set broken bones, so please don't tell me how to write. And I certainly don't need your so called help." Tricia rose from the sofa and stood before him.

"You seem to want to call all the moves tonight," Randall said, annoyed at her.

"Does that bother you?" Tricia glared at him menacingly, but her voice remained calm. "Does it bother you that you're not in charge of every situation, that you don't get your way all the time?"

"Tricia, you really don't understand this relationship at all, do you?"

"I have work to do. Please leave." she said lifelessly.

"Why are you trying to change the subject?" he demanded angrily.

In reply Tricia merely shrugged her shoulders in a gesture designed to belittle the intensity of his emotions and began to walk away from Randall. "I'm going to do my work."

"Oh, no, you're not!" Randall said angrily, grabbing Tricia by an arm and swinging her around to face him. "You're not going to walk away from me, from us, to turn your back and leave when the going gets tough. Isn't that what you've always done before? Run away?"

"Please leave, you . . . you . . ." Tricia repeated, her voice calm but her face red with indignation.

"What's the matter, Tricia? Can't find the word for your emotion? That's your problem, isn't it? You do some emotions so well, and others so poorly. Grief and guilt—you're a master at those. But anger? That's a tough one for you. Isn't it? I'll bet you have never in your life just lost that careful control, screamed at anyone, or thrown a tantrum, have you, Little Miss Perfection?"

"Go away," she said stiffly without raising her voice.

"No. Not until I tell you what I really think about your story. The love scenes between Katherine and Joshua are shallow, cold, and unfeeling. Love is another emotion you're not very good at."

"What do you know about literature?" she asked arrogantly. "You don't know anything about writing, so don't sit in judgment of me."

"I know a heck of a lot more about writing than you know about love!" he interrupted mockingly. "At least I know good writing when I read it. You wouldn't know love if it were standing in front of you." There was a heavy pause as they stared into each other's eyes, each seeing something they had not seen there before. "That's why you can't write about love. You don't know what it is."

"Please go away," Tricia repeated tonelessly, her body trembling and her mind reeling in reaction to his well-aimed barbs. "Please just go away from here."

"My pleasure," he said smugly. "The sooner I'm away from you for good, the better it will be." He walked over to the table where his coat lay and jerked it upward. A glittering flash in the lamplight showed something small and shiny fly from the pocket.

Tricia and Randall both watched in stunned silence as the brilliant diamond engagement ring fell clattering onto the glass tabletop.

Randall walked slowly toward it, picked it up, and held it for a moment between his thumb and first finger, examining it as if it had fallen from the sky. He spoke solemnly. "You asked me to go away, Tricia, and I will. This time it's final. I won't come crawling back again."

Then Tricia watched him walk toward the door, open it calmly, and walk out. Next she heard his car start, and the sound of wheels spinning as he drove away.

"I hate you!" Tricia screamed aloud as a dam inside her seemed to break open and spill a flood of emotions into her body despite her resolve to remain calm. It was as if a volcano had suddenly come to life within her, violently spewing hot, primitive emotions. "I believed in you! I thought you were different! I thought you loved me!" She stormed into the kitchen, picked up a plate waiting to be washed, and threw it across the room, smashing it against a wall. And she realized that it made her feel better.

An hour later Randall's phone rang.

"Hello," he answered curtly, wishing he had thought to have his service screen his calls this evening.

"Randall," came Emily's voice from the telephone, with an unmistakable note of alarm.

"What is it, Emily?" he asked his sister impatiently.

"I'm over at Tricia's house. She called me, asked if I had any bandages. She said she had cut her hand on a broken plate."

"Emily," he said irritably, "if this is one of your schemes, I'm not in the mood to put up with it."

"Randall, she doesn't even know I'm calling you. She needs stitches or something. The gash is really deep, and we can't get it to stop bleeding. Should I drive her to the emergency room at the hospital?"

Randall thought of the possibility of a clash with Tricia in public, of how interested the hospital staff would be, of how they'd gossip. "No. I'll gather what I need and drive over. You stay with her until I get there."

Randall hung up the phone and sighed wearily.

When Randall stood face-to-face with Tricia, whose hand was wrapped in a blood-soaked towel, neither spoke. Emily stood by in awkward confusion, clearly reading anger in both their faces.

"Let's go to the table in the breakfast room," he said brusquely after a quick examination of the wound. "The light there is good, and I'll need a flat surface. There's plenty of work to be done on that hand."

Tricia winced inwardly at his words, but she gave no outward signs of her emotions.

"How did you do this?" he asked without emotion.

"I broke a plate."

"Follow me," he ordered, making his way across the room.

Tricia sat with her arm extended across the table toward Randall.

"Emily, please get me a large bowl or basin half filled with lukewarm water. We'll have to soak this first, to be sure it's clean."

"In the kitchen," Tricia directed, attempting to calm

her voice and conceal her anger and fear. "In the cabinet above the refrigerator."

Emily left the room, and Randall glared at Tricia. "So?" he asked suspiciously, examining again the deep gash on her hand between her thumb and first finger, "you broke a plate?"

"I broke eight plates, to be exact," she answered sarcastically. "Eight plates and five cups."

"That's thirteen." He smirked. "An unlucky number."

"Eight plates, five cups, three saucers, and two soup bowls. I threw them across the room, against a wall. I was cleaning up the mess when this happened."

"Tricia," came Emily's alarmed voice as she reentered the room with the basin Randall had requested. "What happened in there?"

"It seems our princess had her first temper tantrum," Randall answered mockingly. He took the basin from Emily and added some antiseptic from his bag to the water. "Soak it," he directed abruptly.

Tricia hesitated. "Will it burn?"

"Don't be such a baby," he said acidly, forcing her hand into the liquid. "I do this with little children all the time."

"I'm going back into the kitchen to clean up," Emily said uncomfortably. "Call out if you need me. Either of you." She looked at both Tricia and Randall as they glared at each other with hostile stares.

Randall reached into his black bag again, and this time he withdrew a small vial, a long needle, and a syringe.

Tricia paled, then bit her bottom lip.

"I have a good deal of work to do here, and I don't

intend to have to go next door and get Bradley to hold you down. Is that what you want?''

Tricia, totally humiliated by his tone and by her dependence on him, held her wounded left hand out toward him and laid her face in the crook of her right arm, which was resting on the tabletop.

''That's good,'' he continued mockingly. ''Just lie still, hide your face, and let me do my work. I'll be gracious enough to use a local anesthetic on your hand before I begin to do the repair work. Muscle damage, nerve damage, you did quite a job on yourself here. This may take some time.''

''I hate you, Randall Land,'' she said through gritted teeth as he injected the painkiller.

''Ah, yes. Well, Tricia, you may hate me, but for the moment you need me. Unless, of course, you prefer the alternative of bleeding to death. You seem to have gotten a head start on that option from the look of the towel that was wrapped around your hand.''

He worked in silence for several minutes before he spoke again. ''You've nothing more to say, Tricia? Just that you hate me?''

''No,'' she said after a moment's hesitation to consider, her face still buried in her arm. Tricia felt doubly humiliated. She had placed herself in the hands of a man she despised.

''That's all the fight there is in you, Tricia?'' he asked unmercifully. ''Just a few thrown dishes and one growled semithreat?''

''Leave me alone,'' she pleaded, beginning to feel weak from her injury and from the emotional outburst that had preceded it.

"That's exactly what I intended to do when I left here earlier. But you went to rather exaggerated extremes to get me back.''

"You egotistical, arrogant, chauvinistic..." she struggled for a fitting noun to complete her sentence. "This was an accident.''

"The famous Dr. Sigmund Freud said there are no accidents. You wanted me to come back.''

"I certainly did not. Are you almost finished?'' She was anxious for him to leave, worried about losing her control.

"I'm taking my time to do a careful job and minimize the scar. My beautiful lady doesn't want a scar, does she?'' Randall asked sarcastically.

"Don't call me that.''

"What? Beautiful or a lady?''

"How long must I endure this?'' Tricia asked helplessly.

"Not much longer. Just a few more stitches, then I'll bandage it. Are you listening to me?''

"Yes.''

"Keep this hand dry and clean. You can change the bandage if you wish. Try not to use the hand any more than is absolutely necessary. If it becomes very red and swollen or if you develop a fever, you'll need to see the doctor of your choice. Also, in about five days, the stitches will need to be taken out.''

"I understand,'' she answered quietly, her anger spent, a sense of emptiness, a realization of what she'd done, taking its place. She felt cold and began to shiver slightly.

Randall looked at her, quickly noting the paleness of

her complexion and her trembling. "I'll leave a prescription for some mild pain medication. Don't drive when you're taking it."

"I don't want it."

"But the pain?"

"In a poem I read once, the poet said it's good to feel the pain sometimes. It lets you know you're still alive."

"Were you ever alive, Tricia?" he asked quietly as he finished stitching and began bandaging her hand. "I wonder." He continued to bandage, adding thoughtfully, "Take the pills, Tricia. You can debate the great questions of the universe some other time." He laid a small package of pills and a written prescription on the table.

"Emily finished cleaning your kitchen for you. She came in a little while ago, but you didn't look up, and I motioned for her to go home." Randall sighed with weary resignation. "Now I have to go next door and assure her that you are unharmed, that I controlled myself at least that much. I could see from the expression on her face when she left that she was so angry she wanted to choke me. My own sister has cast me in the role of villain in this travesty of a drama."

"Just go home," Tricia mumbled without lifting her head. "There will be so many questions if you go over there now. I'll think of something to tell her. It will save us both a lot of embarrassment."

"Nonsense," he answered. "Emily's smart. She has this all figured out by now. Emily knows exactly what's going on here. You're the only one who doesn't." With that remark he snapped his case shut with an abruptness that startled Tricia.

"Then tell me."

"You're a smart girl; you'll figure it out sooner or later." He paused before adding, "I hope."

"If you're going to Emily's house, thank her for me," Tricia mumbled, her face still averted from Randall. "And close the door behind you."

The anger that had so completely filled the room and both its occupants an hour before was gone. Without the anger, Randall felt only the frustration of not being able to reach Tricia—he hadn't been able to touch her with understanding, with love, or with anger. The walls she had built were simply too strong for any weapon he possessed.

He understood now that she didn't even know what was happening herself. It wasn't that she was phobic about pain, she was afraid of being hurt. Afraid to take chances of any kind, fearful that she wouldn't be able to handle another loss. She was a person who had reached the saturation level of pain and now avoided it at any cost.

Without her anger, Tricia felt only the return of some very old, very familiar ghosts.

Chapter Nine

W eeks passed, but a strange, aching feeling that was new to Tricia settled on her soul and would not pass. She had felt loss and loneliness many times, but this total devastation affected her inward and outward calm as nothing ever had.

At first Tricia covered the signs of sleepless nights by using heavier makeup. But the fact that something was wrong was undeniable. Not only did Tricia lose sleep, she began to lose weight. She tried to busy herself with her writing, but she often sat for hours without a word appearing on the paper.

Tricia felt closed in, surrounded by physical and emotional walls she could not break through, and despite the cold, wet winter weather, she would often bundle herself and go out for a walk with Nicholas in the park.

Nicholas, who was growing and becoming quite

frisky, seemed to enjoy the outings, but Tricia would return home with an increased sense of isolation.

Once, on the way home from one of these walks on a drizzly gray afternoon, Tricia heard Emily call her name. Looking toward the house next door, Tricia saw Emily wave for her to come over.

"You look cold," Emily greeted her cheerfully. "How about some hot chocolate?"

"Yes, I'd like that," Tricia said, taking off her coat and noticing the unusual quiet of the house. "Where are Bradley and the boys?"

"Oh, Randall called and invited Bradley and the boys to go into Houston for a basketball game at the Summit. I have the whole afternoon to myself."

"That's probably a real treat for you."

"Yes, but the house is just too quiet. I'm not used to it." She poured two mugs of hot chocolate and walked toward the table as she spoke. "Tricia," she said in a serious tone as she sat across from her at the table, "is something wrong?"

"Wrong? What do you mean?"

"Have you been sick? You look awful. I don't mean to sound rude, but I'm concerned. Your eyes are sunken. You're as skinny as a skeleton. The lights are on at your house until all hours of the night. You never come to visit the boys anymore."

"Oh, Emily. I'm sorry about the boys."

"We both know that's not the point, Tricia. Bradley and I are worried about you."

"Thank you, Emily, but there's no need to worry. I'm not sick."

"Are you sure? Have you seen Randall?"

"Randall?" Tricia asked defensively. "No. Why should I see Randall?"

"Because he's your doctor," Emily answered simply.

"No. I haven't seen Randall, and I don't plan to. No," she repeated.

"Well, then go and see someone else," Emily suggested, surmising the reason behind Tricia's refusal. "You know another doctor, don't you? From before you moved here?"

"Of course I know other doctors."

"Then you ought to go and see one of them."

"I don't know, Emily," Tricia answered uncertainly. "I'm not ill."

"Call for an appointment, Tricia, before whatever's wrong gets worse."

"Well," Tricia said noncommittally, "there's Vince."

"Then at least you can be sure that you aren't ill. Maybe he can give you something to help you sleep."

"Okay, Emily," Tricia said, biting her bottom lip nervously. "I'll do it."

"Good," Emily said with relief. "Now, let's talk about something else, something more pleasant."

"May I ask you a personal question?" Tricia asked hesitantly.

"I guess I owe you that after all the times I've stuck my nose into your business."

"Emily, how did you know that Bradley was the man you wanted to marry?" Tricia asked.

Emily smiled. "Oh, Tricia. I know some people have to puzzle over that question, but for me it was simple. Bradley was the one bright star in an otherwise pale universe. And given all the other options of a lifetime, I knew that I could spend all my days and nights in Bradley's arms and never feel cheated, as long as at the end of it, I could die in his arms.''

"Oh, Emily, that's beautiful." Tricia sighed.

"I've never regretted it, not for a minute. It's wonderful to know that I am the center of another person's existence, and he is the center of mine. It's like a planet revolving around the sun.''

"I hope that someday I can be that happy."

"The way I see it, happiness isn't the elusive quality people make it out to be. Happiness is simply a matter of knowing what you want, then not changing your mind once you get it.''

"It can't be that simple," Tricia said with misery in her voice. "Not for me, anyway."

"How long are you going to go on like this?" Emily asked kindly.

"Like what?"

"Punishing yourself. Tricia, Randall told me you were avoiding personal relationships because you feel guilty about the accidental death of your fiancé.''

"Randall talks too much," she said without an effort to defend herself against the charge.

"Don't be so hard on him, Tricia. Despite the way he acted the night you cut your hand, Randall really cares about you.''

"He does?" she asked, almost afraid to believe. "He told you that?"

"No. He didn't come right out and say anything about his feelings for you, but he's the kind of person who cares about other people.''

"I see," Tricia said slowly, the disappointment apparent in her voice. She acknowledged to herself that caring for someone had several meanings, several levels of meaning.

"He said that you're extremely intelligent; that you've read everything."

"That's Uncle Jim's doing," she said, musing.

"Uncle Jim?"

"Yes. When I was young he'd read to me. It was something we'd do together every day. Then as I grew older, we'd both read a book and we'd discuss it." She paused. "He's a professor of literature."

"And Randall thinks you're talented."

"Aunt Barbara."

"And beautiful."

"Mother."

"Oh, Tricia, stop it. He knows you're thoughtful and kind and that you care about other people. Now, you can't give anyone else credit for that."

"Oh, Emily," Tricia said sadly, "the only thing I can take credit for is confusing everything, alienating Randall."

"Tricia, believe me, once you feel better physically, everything will seem brighter."

"I hope you're right."

Later that evening Tricia called Vince Johnson and asked if he could see her in his office the next day.

"Patty Ann, you're not ill, are you, dear? You looked beautiful the night of the party, quite healthy."

"Just a little under the weather," she mumbled in reply.

"How's Randall?" he asked cheerfully. "I haven't

heard from him since the party, though that doesn't surprise me. I understand the responsibility of being a small-town MD takes most of his time.''

''I don't know how he is,'' she muttered. ''I haven't seen him in some time.''

''A lovers' quarrel?'' he asked, his voice alive with sudden interest.

''It's not what you think, Vince,'' she answered miserably. ''May I come by tomorrow?''

''Of course, dear. What time would be good for you?''

''I have classes tomorrow. They'll be over about three or four. I could get to your office a little before five.''

''Come by then,'' he said. ''See you tomorrow.''

The next evening Tricia arrived at Vince Johnson's office to find that the nurses had already gone home for the day. Vince, wearing an expensive, attractive suit, sat alone in the empty reception area, waiting for her.

''Ah, Tricia.'' He smiled as she walked in. ''I'm starving. Let's go and have dinner.''

''But . . . but . . .'' she stuttered, uncomprehending.

''Come along,'' he said, taking her firmly by the arm. ''I have reservations for five o'clock. Luckily we're close by.''

Wordlessly she followed his lead.

Tricia found herself sitting across the table from Vince, moving her food around on her plate absent-mindedly. Vince made endless small talk while he ate, then, finally, he asked, ''Well, Patty Ann, or it's Tricia now, isn't it? What seems to be the problem?''

''Here?'' she asked in amazement, her eyes sweeping the room.

"I'm not going to undress you, dear. And it's much more comfortable here than in my office. It's my guess you called me as much as an old friend as a doctor. After all, there are doctors in Asheville. You wouldn't have driven all this way to see me about a cut finger or a common cold."

"No, I guess not," Tricia mused to herself.

"So?"

Tricia moved the food around on her plate for the hundredth time. "I don't feel well. I'm not sleeping."

"And I can see that you have no appetite," Vince added. "Also, you're much too quiet to be a good dinner partner. Let me ask you a few questions. Do you have any obvious symptoms of disease or injury? Headaches? Stomach problems? Fever? Bleeding?"

"No."

He paused thoughtfully. "You say you're having trouble sleeping. Do you wake up in the middle of the night with an empty, aching feeling?"

"Oh, yes," she answered, relieved that he understood.

"And you're having trouble concentrating, keeping your mind on your work?"

"Yes."

"You are suffering from a very common disease, Patty Ann, and the remedy is a simple, time-proven prescription."

"It is?" she asked with obvious relief.

"Yes, Patty Ann. You are in love. You may be denying it, even to yourself, but that's what is bothering you. My professional advice is that you marry the man and allow yourself to be happy."

"You're making fun of me. That's not very professional. I came to you for help."

"Now, Patty Ann, calm down," he interrupted "I could perform dozens of tests, but I'll wager right now that my first diagnosis is the correct one." He paused, smiling at her in a brotherly manner. "It happens to everyone sooner or later. I've often wondered when it would happen to you."

"You're serious?" she asked in disbelief.

"Absolutely. You know Steven and I worked closely together. I knew what was going on, the truth about the two of you. In fact, we argued about it once. This may seem unkind, but maybe it's time to face the facts. Steven didn't love you, Patty Ann. He was seeking a way to forget his wife. And you didn't love him. You respected him, perhaps, and I'm certain you liked him. But love? I didn't see love in your eyes when you looked at each other." He paused, observing Tricia's reactions to his words. "Anyway, I urged him not to marry you, not to waste your beauty and charm, not to waste your youth, to let you fall in love like the rest of humankind."

Tricia continued to stare at him blankly, her mind a puzzle of confused thoughts beginning to take shape. "Why are you telling me this now?" she asked softly.

"So that you'll get on with your life. Forget Steven. Forget Bubba. Forget the past. Get on with your life. Marry Randall and have a few children."

"M . . . mar . . . marry Randall . . ." she stammered. "Why? How did you know?"

"The party New Year's Eve." He smiled broadly. "The magic I didn't see in your eyes when you were with Steven, it was there. I knew Randall in medical school. You two are made for each other.''

''Marry Randall?'' she repeated in a little awestruck voice.

''Sure. He had the same look in his eyes. You moved away to find a new life, Patty Ann. You've been lucky enough to find the right man to share that new life with. Randall told me that you were the most intriguing woman he had ever met.''

''Randall told you that?''

''Yes. And much more.''

''And you told him. . . . ''

''A few things. There was so much about you he didn't know. You had done a pretty good job of covering your past. He seemed relieved to finally know the truth. He loves you, Patty Ann.''

Tricia sat quietly for a few minutes, considering his words. ''Thank you, Vince,'' she said in a low tone.

''Whatever for?''

''You've answered a great many questions I've been asking myself.''

''Patty Ann, it was my pleasure. Now, shall I take you back to your car?''

On the drive back home, Tricia thought of everything Vince had told her. And she thought about Emily, of how Emily had described Bradley as ''the one bright star in an otherwise pale universe.'' Tricia saw her mistake.

This must be love, she thought to herself. *It seems strange, no doubt, but this must be love.*

She now had the answers to her questions, but new questions blossomed in her mind like wildflowers in the springtime. How could she tell Randall? Would he want to know? Or could it be too late? Tricia knew that she must be able to think clearly before she acted again. She didn't dare make another mistake.

The sun set, and as Tricia arrived home and walked into her house, she heard the clock strike nine. Despite the early hour, she fixed herself a snack, then went to bed and slept until, once again, the clock was striking nine. She awakened to a clear, cloudless day and a ravenous appetite. It was as if she had slept and upon awakening found a new world, a world of confidence, not fear, a world void of past tragedies and shining with bright new promise.

Every Wednesday Randall closed his office at noon and spent the afternoon with his patients in the nursing home. Some needed medical attention, others just the reassurance that they were in good health. His visits often saved them from having to go out in inclement weather to see him at the office. Today he had received an urgent message from Harry asking Randall to come by his room.

Wonder what the old man is up to this time, Randall thought as he tapped on the door to Harry's room.

"Randall," Harry began seriously after Randall had seated himself. "I've known you since you were a young boy, since you used to deliver my newspapers. I feel that I can talk freely to you, like a father to a son."

"I'm pleased that you feel that way, Harry," Randall said encouragingly.

"I'll be blunt. You need to get married. You're too

old to be single. You need to have children. Get married before you're too old and set in your ways.''

''Married?'' Randall asked in mild surprise. ''That would require the cooperation of a woman. Who is it I should marry?'' he asked, humoring the old man.

''There are lots of nice girls.'' Harry walked with a tottering step to the door of his room and opened it. The sound of moderately talented singing voices could be heard from the main room. ''There are the Hudson sisters. They all have lovely voices,'' he suggested calculatingly.

Randall winced at the thought. ''Harry,'' he began tactfully, ''Bernice is much too old for me. Clarisse has already been married unsuccessfully half a dozen times. That's usually an indication of a woman I'd like to avoid. Hanna is already married. I'm afraid that eliminates the Hudson sisters. And ''—Randall cleared his throat uncomfortably—''they are not really my type.''

''Well, then,'' Harry said, rubbing his face as if in deep concentration. ''There's Tricia,'' he suggested hopefully, as if the thought had suddenly come to him.

''Ah,'' Randall said, the true intentions of Harry's request that he visit today becoming clear. ''You think that I should marry Tricia McGill.''

''Tricia McGill, yes, I think you should,'' he affirmed.

''Why do you want me to marry her?''

Harry suddenly came to life. ''Because she's beautiful, Randall, and sweet and talented. She's exactly the right girl for you.'' He spoke as if he were selling a used car. ''Besides, she owns my house,'' Harry said, getting to the real point of the issue. ''It isn't safe for a house to be with just a woman. There should be a man to look after things. You're almost like a son to me. I want you to live in my house.''

Randall saw the conviction in the old man's eyes, and he was genuinely sorry he could not oblige him. "I took Tricia out a few times," he said softly. "We agreed not to do it again. Our last encounter was especially unpleasant. I'm sure she wouldn't want to see me again.''

"Couldn't you try her one more time? Be sincere: women like sincerity," Harry advised.

Randall shook his head slowly. "You said that Tricia is beautiful, Harry, and she is. She's like a china doll, lovely to look at, but cold, detached, unfeeling. And that smooth exterior never cracks. Always the same—unruffled. Maybe that's what bothers me most about her. Real people have real emotions, pleasant or unpleasant, but emotions. Not Tricia. She's like the doll on the shelf that you can look at and admire, but never touch, never get close to.''

The old man looked at him in dismay. "You're trying to tell me you can't love Tricia because she never gets mad?''

"She never gets anything, Harry. Not mad, not glad. I can't reach her.''

"Try again.''

"I'm sorry, Harry," he replied, patting the old man's shoulder affectionately as he rose to go. "But we agreed, and I really don't see any way around it. She wouldn't agree to it, either. When I left she told me to close the door on my way out. I think she meant it figuratively as well as literally. To close the door on our relationship.''

"Why?''

"Neither of us knew what we were getting into. Neither was prepared. I think fate was against us."

"Humbug!" Harry scoffed irritably. "What is wrong with the two of you? I know you're right for each other. I haven't lived this long without learning a few things. Believe me, love isn't something you can prepare for. It's something that just happens. And then only if you're lucky. And it won't just go away if you ignore it. We're not talking about the three-day measles here, Randall. We're talking about a lifetime commitment."

"I stay so busy with my work. I could hardly be fair."

"You," he sputtered angrily. "If you're too busy for love, you're too darned busy!"

"Harry," Randall said soothingly.

"Go away. Leave me alone. You make me mad when you talk like a darned fool. Go away."

"Very well," Randall said, turning and walking slowly from the room. It seemed to him that lately everyone was telling him to go away.

Chapter Ten

Morning dawned clear, bright, frosty, and crisp, an exact replica of the days before it. In fact, since Tricia had acknowledged her feelings for Randall, the weather seemed to mirror her emotions.

Tricia hummed to herself as she did her routine household chores, fed the dog, and watered the plants. Although she hadn't yet talked to Randall, she felt confident that things could be worked out between them. After all, she told herself, Emily had said that happiness was just a simple matter of getting what you want, then not changing your mind. Tricia assured herself that in the past she hadn't been sure of exactly what she wanted. Now that she was sure, she'd get it. She decided that she'd call Randall today after he closed his office and invite him for dinner.

The ringing of the telephone startled her from these thoughts.

"Hello?"

"Tricia, this is Mrs. Turner from Dr. Land's office," came a hurried and agitated voice.

"What's wrong? Has something happened?" Tricia asked with a feeling of terrible premonition.

"It's Harry Lindow. They think he's had another heart attack. He's being rushed to the hospital. Tricia, he's asking for you."

"I'm on my way," Tricia volunteered before being asked, her own heart beating irregularly with panic.

Grabbing a coat on the way out to the car, Tricia raced to the hospital, found the emergency entrance, and made her way in.

A nurse in a starched white uniform ushered Tricia into the cardiac care room where Harry lay in a bed, covered to his waist, his bare chest exposed except for the numerous wires that led to machines that registered information and displayed it in various visual and audio forms for the doctors and nurses to interpret.

A blood pressure cuff was wrapped around his left arm, and his eyes were closed. A sudden thought that perhaps Harry had died before she could arrive was quickly dismissed as she noted the sounds emitting from the equipment.

Tricia went quietly to the bedside and took Harry's hand in hers. "Harry," she said softly, "Harry. It's me, Tricia. I'm here."

Harry slowly opened his eyes. "Tricia," he whispered, barely audible. "Tricia, stay with me."

"I will, Harry. I'll stay right here with you for as long as you need me." Absorbed in Harry's tragedy, Tricia did not notice Randall standing on the far side of the bed with a puzzled expression on his face, interpreting information from the equipment, reading and rereading test results.

As Randall puzzled over Harry's condition, Tricia leaned over the elderly man, softly murmuring words of comfort and encouragement. After a time, Randall turned toward them and stared intently for a few, thoughtful minutes. Then he turned to the nurses. "Would you leave us alone?"

Hearing Randall's voice startled Tricia. She knew that Randall would be the attending physician, but her attention had been focused on Harry.

The nurses, nodding their assent, left the room quietly, Tricia looked around, unsure if she should follow. "No, Tricia, you stay," Randall instructed.

Randall took a step toward Harry's bed. "Harry," he said seriously, "is there something you want us to do? Any last request?"

Tricia gasped aloud in shock. What kind of doctor was Randall? To tell Harry that he was dying and to do nothing to prevent it? She noted to herself that Randall hadn't administered any medications to Harry, hadn't tried to help him. Could Randall be that callous? Could she have misjudged him so badly?

Reading the shock on Tricia's upturned face, Randall suggested, "Sit down, Tricia. Pull a chair up to Harry's bed."

"I think I'll stand," she retorted sharply, feeling the anger grow inside her. "I may have to run get medical attention for him." How could he be so insensitive? Did he really expect her to be a part of it?

"Well," Harry? Randall asked.

"Randall," Harry whispered weakly. "Tricia. Please, take hold of each other's hands, across the bed, over me."

Tricia felt that she could do little but comply with Harry's rather odd request. She reluctantly extended her hand to Randall. Randall took Tricia's hand as Harry opened his eyes narrowly to see that it had been done, then closed them quickly again. "Now, look into each other's eyes."

Still following Harry's directions, Tricia looked up toward Randall, but with still greater shock she saw him grinning broadly, as if he was actually amused at the scene.

Tricia's mouth fell open, and she started to say something, to rebel against Randall's heartless attitude, but he raised a finger to his lips in a gesture to silence her.

"Have you done it? Are you looking into each other's eyes?" Harry asked.

"Yes, Harry," Randall said in a serious tone that belied his facial expression.

"Now," Harry said in a voice barely above a whisper, "confess your true feelings for each other, that you're both in—"

Tricia, unable to contain her contempt for Randall any longer, sputtered angrily. "I think you are the most despicable, intolerable, incompassionate, sadistic beast I have ever known or even heard of. You're a charlatan, and if anything happens to Harry—"

Harry's eyes flew open and he sat instantly upright in the bed as Tricia spoke, his eyes wide with amazement.

"It's all right, Harry," Randall said jovially, taking

his hand from Tricia's and patting Harry affectionately on the back. "It was a noble effort, but the act's over. I'm onto you, Harry. Congratulations on a wonderful performance. You almost had me fooled."

"Darn," Harry said, suddenly and completely recovered. "Double darn. I was sure it would work."

Tricia, totally astonished at the sudden revelation, collapsed into a chair, trying to regain her composure as Randall helped Harry free himself from the complicated machinery that ensnarled him. He helped Harry out of bed and into his shirt. She sat, numbed, not listening, as they spoke. She tried to put the events of the last half hour into some kind of logical perspective.

Finally she heard Randall say, "The nurses will help you get checked out while I have a word with this beautiful woman here. Then, maybe, if she isn't too angry with you, she'll drive you home."

Randall called for a nurse, who helped Harry from the room.

Randall watched the exodus, then turned, smiling amiably, toward Tricia. "Another one of Harry's tricks. I hope you weren't too alarmed. He didn't mean to harm anyone."

Tricia, still overwhelmed, looked up at him. "You knew? You knew what Harry was doing?"

"Yes, Tricia. Not at first, of course, but after reading all the data, then recalling an earlier conversation we'd had, I realized what he was up to."

"I'm so sorry for the awful things I said," Tricia apologized. "I should have had more faith in you."

"I suppose I deserve them. I wanted to warn you, but

there just wasn't any way.'' He smiled at her discomfort. ''You couldn't have known,'' he said.

''But the things I said. Oh, Randall.'' Once again, Tricia regretted the harsh words she had spoken to him. ''It seems like every time I open my mouth around you I say the wrong things! I stay perfectly calm and poised around other people without any problem. But around you it's different. You make me sad. You make me mad.''

''I make you feel, Tricia,'' he said. ''I make you a real person, not a decoration. The capacity to experience emotions is one of the things that sets us apart from inanimate objects. Real people have feelings.''

''But sometimes, around you, it's so overwhelming.''

''It's all right, Beautiful. I understand,'' he said, putting his arms loosely around her shoulders and drawing her near.

''I wish you wouldn't call me beautiful,'' she said softly, her hands against his chest, feeling the strength there.

Randall paused thoughtfully before replying. ''When I saw you with Harry, the expression on your face when you thought he was dying showed me that caring was beautiful. Whenever I see you with Emily's boys, how they drop everything to run to you when they see you outside, how they fight for your attention, then I know beauty is not found here,'' he said, tracing the outline of her face. ''It's here,'' he said, lightly placing his hand on the center of her chest. ''It's in your heart.''

''I'm beautiful on the inside?'' she asked in disbelief.

''Yes, Tricia,'' he answered, his voice a caress.

''No one ever told me that before.''

Randall took both Tricia's hands in his, and, raising them to his lips, kissed them. "There are many things I'd like to tell you, things I hope no one has ever said to you before." Once again, he kissed the hands he held. Then his attention went to the small scar on her left hand. "Your hand healed well," he said, examining it, trying to forget the terrible events of the fateful evening when he had been called to treat the wound.

Tricia steadied her gaze on Randall's eyes. "Randall," she said softly, "I need to apologize . . . to explain to you. How can I ask you to forgive me, except to say that I was held by ghosts of the past and that I will not allow them to haunt me any longer. They made me helpless. I want to be a whole person."

Randall looked at Tricia uncertainly, trying to absorb the full meaning of what she was saying to him, when suddenly a loudspeaker above them came to life.

"Dr. Land, please report to the emergency room," a voice boomed from the speaker. "Dr. Land, please report to the emergency room."

"Dr. Land—that's me," he said hesitantly, looking around, as if he were searching for an avenue of escape.

"You're busy," Tricia said, allowing him to follow where his duty led him.

"Yes. I'm too darned busy," Randall said bitterly, recalling Harry's earlier admonishment: *If you're too busy for love, you're too darned busy.*

To Tricia, who wasn't aware of the earlier conversation, the words implied he was too busy for her, for them, for what she was offering, what he too had once wanted. His words stung like an unexpected slap in the face. She drew in a sharp breath, turned quickly, and began to walk away before she could react visibly to his words. He may have allowed her to make a fool of herself, confessing her emotions to a man who didn't have the time nor the inclination to care, but he wouldn't have the satisfaction of seeing how much it hurt.

"Tricia." His voice called from behind her. "Tricia, listen to me, I. . . . "

The rest of his words were drowned out by the voice on the speaker paging him again.

Blinking back tears, Tricia turned the corner to find Harry, seated comfortably, waiting for her to drive him back to the nursing home.

"Well, Harry," she murmured softly, choking on her words, "we're lucky. This was just a false alarm." *I'm lucky I found out what he's really like,* she thought to herself, *before. . . . Before what?* she asked herself. *Before I fall in love with him? It's too late for that!*

As she drove across town, Harry spoke for the first time.

"I'm sorry if I worried you, Tricia. Do you understand why I did this?"

"I think I do, Harry," she said after a moment's thought. "You don't belong in that institution. You aren't ill. You feel abandoned by your own son. You may even feel caged there, isolated from the life you knew. You miss your home, your old way of life, your independence."

"Tricia," Harry interrupted, surprised that she hadn't guessed the truth.

"No, Harry, let me finish. You're not going to stay there anymore. I'm going to move you into the guest house, if that's agreeable to you. I'll have it repaired. It shouldn't take too long. Then you'll have your yard again, your garden. You can take your walks in the park, just like before you were sick. You can visit with the neighbors, or have your privacy. And I'll be there if you need anything, or if you get sick or lonely.''

''You'd do that for me?'' he asked in surprise.

''Yes, Harry. We single folks have to watch out for each other.''

''I thought today was a failure,'' he muttered to himself, ''and in a way it was. Still, who would have thought it would end like this?'' Harry then turned to Tricia. ''I have, from the day I met you, felt a sense of kinship with you. Now you've proven to be much more than family. You're also a great friend.''

''Harry, whatever happened to your family?''

''My wife died six years ago.''

''And your son?''

''Worthless.'' Harry seemed to feel that this simple, one-word reply would fully explain the complex, mangled relationship.

Tricia did not push for details, but her silence hung in the air until Harry continued.

''Twenty-two years ago, when John was much younger, he fathered a child, *my grandchild,* but he abandoned the mother and wouldn't claim the child.''

Harry seemed saddened as he framed his thoughts in order to present a complete, accurate picture. ''When I found out, we argued about it. He said that he just did not want the responsibility of raising a child.''

''What did you do?''

''After I tired of arguing with John, I tried to contact the young woman without John's knowledge. I thought she might need some help. If John wouldn't help her, my wife and I would.''

''What was she like?''

Harry frowned in concentration. ''It's hard to say. I only met her a few times, and it was so long ago.'' He searched his memory, rubbing his forehead as he did so. ''She was pretty, young, and blond. I could see why John was attracted to her.''

''Did you ever find her?''

''Too late,'' Harry answered mournfully. ''When I finally located members of her family, I learned that I was too late. The mother had moved away! I never knew what became of her.''

''And the child?''

''They wouldn't give me any information, not a crumb.'' Some time passed and then Harry sighed heavily. ''My son and I have committed one of the classic mistakes,'' he remarked morosely.

''What is that?''

''We haven't learned to accept each other for what we are. I just wanted John to be responsible, to settle down. To accept the consequences of what he'd done and try to make the relationship work, to give it a chance.''

''And what is it about you that John can't accept?'' Tricia asked, unable to comprehend the ruptured relationship.

''John wants me to be silent and opinionless.''

''Silent and opinionless.'' Tricia couldn't help but see the irony in the situation. ''Those two adjectives do not describe you, Harry, nor would I want them to.''

After settling Harry back into his room, Tricia returned home. The phone rang intermittently throughout the evening, but Tricia stubbornly refused to answer it. She did not want to speak to Randall, to make a fool of herself, ever again.

Chapter Eleven

Days passed. The old gloom that had invaded Tricia's life after her argument with Randall, then dissipated after her talk with Vince, returned. Tricia busied herself hiring and overseeing the work of carpenters, plumbers, painters, and decorators, seeing that the guest cottage was made ready for Harry to move into.

But the construction wasn't the only work to be done. Harry's furniture had to be taken out of storage and brought to his new home.

"Well," Tricia murmured to herself, fumbling with the keys, "let's hope this one works." She tried the last key on the ring and heard the snap of the lock opening. Tricia leaned into the heavy door as it squeaked its protest at being opened after a year of undisturbed rest.

Tricia groped for a light switch as her eyes slowly became accustomed to the dark, dusty storage room. She found the switch, but after one glance at the chaos of the warehouse, she regretted her success.

Whoever had removed Harry's things from the house before she bought it had been careless, hasty, or uncaring. Pieces of furniture lay haphazardly atop each other. Opened and unopened boxes were scattered about.

Tricia had hired two teenage boys to help her move the heavy pieces of furniture the next day, but she was glad she'd come alone today. There was plenty of work to be done sorting through Harry's belongings, deciding what would be needed to turn the guest house into Harry's home. The cluttered arrangement would make the task even more difficult and time-consuming. Tricia began by surveying the larger items and listing what would be taken from storage. There was certainly more than enough furniture here to fill several buildings the size of her guest cottage.

"The small dining table and chairs," she said to herself as she began the list. "The oak bed and dresser for the bedroom. Harry's leather recliners and the big braided rug for the front of the fireplace." Tricia scribbled down each item as she named it, visualizing how it would look in the newly painted and papered rooms. "Now the more personal things—curios for the shelves and fireplace mantel, the books Harry asked for, bed covers, towels. . . . " Tricia sighed to herself and rolled up her sleeves before beginning the enormous task. Half overwhelmed, half grateful for the opportunity to stay busy and keep her mind from wandering off onto subjects she'd rather forget, Tricia resolved to begin with the box nearest her and work her way toward the back of the room.

Hours later and on the third page of her list, Tricia located a box labeled BOOKS. She reached into her pocket for the list of titles Harry had asked for. Kneeling on the dusty floor, Tricia began stacking the books as she found them. Concentrating on the books to be sorted, Tricia didn't notice the stack growing precariously high until her elbow brushed against it, sending the books tumbling noisily across the floor and causing her heart to race.

"I'll pick these up, then go home," Tricia told herself, looking out the door and seeing the sun setting on the horizon. She realized that she'd spent more time than she had planned alone in an isolated warehouse just outside the city limits. Anxious to be safe in her home, Tricia grabbed the fallen books from the dirty concrete floor. As she reached for a leatherbound volume of Faulkner's short stories, a flutter of paper sailing downward caught Tricia's eye.

Tricia picked up the paper, noting that it wasn't a page torn from the binding of the dog-eared book. A man's small, firm handwriting flowed across the page.

Without thought Tricia scanned the yellowed letter. It was a note to Harry from his son, John. As Tricia began to fold it and put it away, something caught her attention. Laura. That was her mother's name. *There are many people named Laura,* Tricia assured herself. Still, she dropped the armload of books she was holding onto a mattress nearby and sat wearily in a chair to read the letter more carefully. The date in the upper right corner told Tricia that the letter was written the year of her birth.

Dad,
    I'm leaving before you awaken because I don't

*want another argument that won't settle the prob-
lem anyway. I know I've made mistakes—mistakes
for which I've paid dearly, and, it seems, continue
to pay. Please accept that it's too late for me to
marry Laura and raise the baby together as you
wish.*

John

Ignoring the mess around her, Tricia stumbled from
the room, into her car, and drove home, still clutching
the now-rumpled letter in her hand.

A few days later, Tricia went out to look over the
cottage, which was nearly ready for Harry to move into.
Thanks to Tricia's hard work in the warehouse, the cottage was now completely furnished with his own things.
His leather armchairs sat in the main room waiting for
him. The tiled floor had been polished, and large rugs as
well as carefully chosen wallpaper gave the room a
warm, masculine look. Harry's own books lined the
shelves, and photographs of his family and friends
perched on the mantelpiece. Soon he would be sleeping
in his own bed again.

Everything had been chosen for Harry's comfort. The
entire cottage reflected his personality. Looking around,
Tricia could almost see Harry sitting in one of the armchairs, his shoulders slumped from years of hard, honest
labor. His gnarled, arthritic hands wrapped around a
book or holding a pipe, his wrinkled face alight with
some imagined or remembered mischief. Thinking of
him, Tricia smiled with fond affection.

It came to her suddenly and with frightening clarity

that physical beauty didn't have the importance she had always attached to it. A mutually loving, protecting relationship had nothing to do with appearance. It seemed so simple now. How could she have not seen it before? The revelation of this simple truth stunned her, and she was forced to stand back at a distance and view her own life from a different perspective.

She had loved her mother, and her mother had been beautiful. But she had not loved her mother because of her beauty. She had loved her for her patience, her smile, for the time they had spent together. For the first time Tricia realized that there was absolutely no proof that the man who had ended her mother's life had been lured there by her beauty. Perhaps he had killed her for some other sick, angry reason, completely unassociated with her mother's looks.

And Steven. *He loved me in his own way,* she thought, though she had to admit that he had not been physically attracted to her. This had been a great puzzle to Tricia in light of the way other men had treated her, but now she saw it all clearly. Steven had looked into her soul, and he had seen a friend there. A friend was all he demanded. A friendship was all they had.

People love each other for what is inside, Tricia concluded.

But still the old questions gnawed at her. *Then why?* came the question that had eaten away at her these last few years. Why had men treated her the way they had? Strange men, who had made unwelcomed advances toward her. She had shied away from these men, instinctively knowing that no relationship at all was preferable to one based solely on physical attraction.

What's the answer? she asked herself. *What is it I'm missing?*

Feeling that she was on the brink of some great discovery, Tricia bent to pick up Nicholas, who was nipping at her heels, and encouraged her mind to explore, to reach out, to discover. She closed her eyes and stroked the puppy's soft fur.

She thought of the people who had been important in her life. Her mother, Aunt Barbara and Uncle Jim, Steven, Emily, and Randall. There her mind stopped and refused to go further. Randall. What was it she felt for him? Love or infatuation? Caring or physical attraction? *Could it be both?* she asked herself in wonder. *Could I have stumbled onto the discovery of a lifetime? Of a million lifetimes?*

While Tricia was lost in these thoughts, Emily walked into the cottage.

''Tricia,'' came Emily's voice from the doorway. ''This place looks great! What are you planning to do with it?''

''Harry Lindow's going to move in,'' Tricia answered, awakened from her thoughts by Emily's voice.

''Harry?''

''He misses his home,'' Tricia added, turning to face her visitor. ''He feels as if he's lost his independence.''

''He told you that?''

''Not exactly,'' Tricia said reflectively. ''There are some things people don't have to say in words.''

''Why do I suddenly feel we're not talking about Harry anymore?'' Emily asked with her usual perceptiveness.

"We are, but not just Harry. Other people have made their feelings clear to me also."

"And you're not happy about that?" Emily guessed.

"I guess it's better I found out now." Tricia paused, then spoke again. "Oh, Emily, do you remember the day we talked about what happiness is?"

"Yes."

"What if a person can't have what they want?"

"Maybe that person should give it another try, a real, honest, all-out effort. Then, if that doesn't work, at least you, I mean that person, knows he or she tried," Emily answered knowingly.

"Another try?"

"Don't give up too easily," Emily advised. "Old Harry obviously didn't. Even after he became ill and sold his home. It must have seemed impossible to him that he'd ever be back. Yet from the look of things, he'll be back puttering about this place, and very soon."

Tricia thought it over, then brightened. "Thanks, Emily. You've given me an idea. I'll do what Harry did." Her heart felt suddenly light.

"Do what Harry did? How?" Emily asked in surprise as Tricia hugged her, then scampered off to her house.

Entering her kitchen, Tricia picked up the telephone and dialed Randall's number, but to her disappointment, his answering service greeted her.

"This is Tricia McGill," she told the operator. "I'd appreciate it if Dr. Land would call me back."

"Are you a patient? Is this an emergency?"

"No. I'm a personal friend."

The service assured her that Randall would receive her message. Then she hung up.

While Tricia waited for Randall to return her call, she returned to the guest house to finish the preparations for its new resident. As she placed dishes in the kitchen cabinet, she heard Harry's voice calling to her from the front room of the cottage.

"I'm in the kitchen, Harry," she called in reply to the beckoning voice. Soon the worn, welcome figure appeared in the doorway. "How do you like it?" she asked, turning around and gesturing at the surroundings.

Harry looked around. "It's beautiful, Tricia, more beautiful than I could have imagined."

Tricia studied Harry's figure, his slumped shoulders and lined face. "Then why aren't you sounding more excited?"

"Why are you doing this for me, Tricia?" he asked meaningfully.

"I like you, Harry. I thought we enjoyed each other's company. And you need a home of your own. You shouldn't be in that facility where you're living now."

"But there must be more to it than that. Everyone is asking questions that I can't answer. My son John has called me more times in the last two weeks than in the year before that. He's worried about me, trying to protect me. He's convinced you're trying to pull some sort of scam, steal my money."

Tricia searched Harry's disturbed countenance. Her own feelings since finding the letter had left her just as uncertain. How much should she tell him? Would it be fair to get his hopes up about something that, for now, was only a suspicion?

"Is there more to this than just my enjoying your company?" she echoed Harry's words, deciding that since half truths had brought about the problems, more half truths would only worsen them. ''Yes and no.''

''What do you mean?'' Harry asked, seating himself at the table.

Tricia joined him, entwining his wrinkled, callused fingers with her long, slender ones. ''Harry, you were honest with me when you told me about your son, John, and your search for your missing grandchild.''

Harry gazed at Tricia intently, trying to read the meaning behind her words.

Tricia hesitated. Did she dare go on? ''I may be that little girl you searched for twenty years ago. If I'm not her, then I am, or was, someone just like her.''

Harry stared at Tricia incredulously.

''I never knew my father,'' Tricia said slowly. ''He never married my mother.''

''Did she die?'' Harry asked meaningfully.

''My mother was murdered,'' Tricia stated simply.

Harry shook his head in shocked disbelief.

''I went to live with an aunt and uncle. The police were concerned about my safety. If anyone had tried to find me, they would have met with fierce opposition from my aunt and uncle and from the authorities.''

''Do you mean that you are . . .'' he asked in a voice filled with awe, the puzzles of the past beginning to take shape.

''I don't know if I am who you think I am. I'm only saying that it's possible. There are certain coincidences. My mother lived here in Asheville for a short time, so theoretically she and John could have met and become attracted to each other. The physical description you gave of the young woman fits my mother's also.''

Harry gazed at her in speechless wonder.

"The girl you wanted John to marry, her name was Laura, wasn't it?"

Harry's brow wrinkled. "Laura . . . Laura . . ." He concentrated. "Yes. It was Laura. A hauntingly beautiful name. It fit her."

"There are many people named Laura," Tricia reminded both Harry and herself.

"Your mother?" he asked anxiously as he began to recover from the surprising news.

"Yes. My mother was named Laura, but I don't know if she was the same Laura whom John loved."

"Then we'll find out. We'll open an investigation."

"And in the meantime, we'll just believe in good fortune, Harry, and that will be enough, won't it?"

"Of course, my dear girl, of course," Harry said, tears of joy shining in his eyes.

A few hours later the phone rang, and Tricia's heart seemed to skip a beat as she reached for it.

"Hello," she answered breathlessly.

"Ms. McGill, this is Dr. Land's answering service. He asked that we call and tell you he's tied up with patients all afternoon, but he'll call you later this evening."

"Thank you," Tricia said, unable to hide her disappointment. Was that just a polite brush-off, or did he really intend to call? Tricia couldn't stand the thought of waiting hours by the phone for a call that didn't come, yet she couldn't leave for fear that she'd miss the call if it did come.

Tricia walked over to where Nicholas played. Seeing her coming, he ran toward her. "Now I know why they say a dog is a man's best friend,'' she told the puppy. ''At least you come when I call you.''

Several hours passed, but Randall still had not called. Noticing the clock, Tricia remembered that his office would be closing soon. ''He's going to talk to me,'' Tricia told herself resolutely. ''If he won't call, I'll go and see him. He can hardly refuse to see a patient!''

When Tricia arrived at Randall's office, only a few patients remained.

''Tricia,'' Mrs Turner beamed when Tricia approached her desk. ''How are you today, dear?''

''I'm fine, Mrs. Turner,'' she said, gathering her courage. ''I'd like to speak with Randall when he's finished with all his patients. Could you arrange that?''

''Sure. I'll tell him you're here.''

''No,'' Tricia stated, looking around to see that no one overheard. ''No. I want it to be a surprise. This is a personal, not a professional, visit.''

''So that's what he's been going around here muttering to himself about these last few days. I should have known!'' Mrs Turner's words were accompanied by a wide, knowing grin. ''I sure hope you can do something to cheer him. I've never seen him act like such a bear.''

Mrs. Turner led her to a treatment room, and Tricia sat uncomfortably, wondering if she was doing the right thing. It wasn't too late yet. She could still walk out. What if she was wrong? What if Randall really did feel that he was too busy for her? What if there was no room in his life for her? What if he didn't love her as he had said he did? What if he was like the others, and not special as she had once thought? What if, despite the opinions of Vince, Harry, Emily, and Aunt Barbara, she and Randall were not right for each other?

Debating with herself, Tricia listened to the sounds of the office. In another room a baby cried, and Tricia thought sympathetically of the infant.

Somewhere in the building the phone rang.

Several times she heard Randall's footsteps in the hall-way, and each time she held her breath and her heart skipped a beat. Finally the footsteps paused on the other side of the closed door to the room in which she sat.

"Mrs. Turner!" she heard Randall call irritably. "Where is the chart on this patient? It's supposed to be on the door."

"I'll get it for you, Dr. Land," Mrs. Turner said calmly. "You just go on in. I'll bring it to you."

Randall opened the door. The look of irritation on his face faded into one of mingled concern and surprise when he saw Tricia.

"Tricia, are you ill?" he asked gently.

"No. Not ill. I'm afraid I've broken something." She found her voice much more uneven than she had expected it to be, and her eyes seemed glued to Randall's face.

Randall's eyes traveled over her quickly, then, unable to notice any obvious injury, he seemed confused. "You've broken a bone?"

"No, you don't understand." She paused briefly, then gathering her courage, she continued. "I think I have a broken heart."

Randall smiled, a small smile of relief and acknowl-edgement, then he spoke. "Well, you've come to the right man.'' He leaned near her. ''What makes you think you have a broken heart? Tell me your symptoms.''

''I can't eat. I can't sleep.''

''You look as if you've lost weight.''

''I have,'' she agreed.

''Do you find yourself thinking about someone special? About all the things you'd like to do with him, for him? About all the places you'd like to go with him, things you'd like to show him? Wondering what could be wrong with him that he can't see what you're feeling?''

''Oh, yes.'' She sighed.

''Have you been irritable and moody?''

''Yes.'' She nodded in agreement.

He pretended to ponder. ''I concur with your diagnosis. You definitely are suffering from a broken heart.''

''And the prognosis?''

''I think there's an excellent chance for recovery, but we'll have to begin your treatment right away. First, I'll prescribe a romantic dinner for two, and then we'll discuss your future course of treatment. I have some very innovative ideas and theories concerning this particular disease. It's an aggressive treatment that you can't get anywhere else.''

''I'd like to hear all about it,'' she murmured as Randall's arms went around her.

The sound of a door slamming shut and a car starting told them that Mrs. Turner had locked the building and gone home for the day.

''I've missed you, Randall,'' she said with tears shining in her blue eyes. ''I've missed you so much.''

Her simple confession caused Randall to lift her gently

from the table and hold her tightly against him, his face resting against her soft, fragrant hair. They stood that way in the quiet building for a long time, each content to hold and be held. "Oh, Princess," he said finally, breaking the long silence. "Do you have any idea what you do to me?"

At dinner Tricia and Randall did little more than smile at each other while their food grew cold. Throughout the meal Tricia found Randall's gentle, wordless caring harder to resist than a physical embrace would have been.

"Oh, Tricia," he said, breaking the heavy silence. "You always seem to be slipping away just when I think I have you in my grasp."

"It doesn't have to be that way," she replied in a tremulous whisper.

"I was afraid you'd disappear before we could straighten this out, just move away, close the door and start over again."

"What good would it have done me to move away? Every time I close my eyes, you'd still be there, inside of me."

"Is what you're saying true, Tricia?"

"I don't believe that I could ever run so far that I could run away from my feelings for you."

After dinner, Randall drove to Tricia's house, and they went inside.

There was an awkward silence. "Tricia," he said finally, taking her hands in his. "I've been wanting to come by here and talk to you about something."

"What?" she asked, noting the seriousness of his tone, the subtle change of mood.

"Harry."

"But you said Harry was okay," she said, concern clear in her features. "You told me he faked his heart attack."

"He's in perfect health."

"What then?"

"The administrators at the home where he lives told me you are making arrangements to have him move out. They said that you talked to his son, that John had finally agreed, and that you plan to move him into the guest cottage behind your house."

"What could possibly be wrong with that? He'll be happier here. He can get out on nice days. He can visit with the neighbors. He can go for his walks in the park. You can't deny that the exercise will be good for his heart. And I'll be here to help him if he becomes ill, or if there's anything he can't handle."

"You're both forgetting something."

"What?"

"This is a very small, conservative town. A young unmarried woman cannot have an older man living with her. People won't understand. It's not respectable."

Tricia looked at Randall. "That's the beauty of it, Randall. He has a grandchild my age somewhere, a grandchild he's never met. You know my background. I may be his granddaughter. There are so many similarities, too many to ignore. We're going to launch an investigation."

"Don't, Tricia," Randall interrupted hastily. "Don't. No good will come from reopening old wounds. It doesn't help the wound heal. It only makes them hurt again.''

Distressed over his attitude, Tricia asked, ''Don't you care about me? About Harry? About our happiness?''

''You know I do.''

''Then why?'' she asked dismally. In the next moment a thought occurred to her. ''You know something, Randall, don't you?''

''Yes,'' he answered. ''There's no need to open an investigation. You are not John Lindow's daughter.''

In reply, Tricia could only stare blankly at him. ''How can you be so sure?'' she finally asked.

''Do you remember I told you that I tried to promote a reconciliation between Harry and his son when Harry was ill?''

''Yes.''

''John told me the truth then. The woman wasn't your mother. It was someone else. She was very young, and very scared. She miscarried early into the pregnancy. Shortly after she moved away from Asheville. John hasn't seen her since.

''John felt terrible after she left. He felt as if he should have married the girl; I believe he really loved her. He was so ashamed of his actions, he couldn't admit his guilt to his father. He allowed Harry to believe that he had simply deserted the girl and his baby. It was easier on both of them.''

Tricia stood speechless, separating the truth from the illusion she had created. Finally she asked, ''What about me, my father?''

''On your birth certificate, who is listed as the father?''

"It says 'unknown.' "

"As difficult as it is, Tricia, you may as well accept the fact that your biological father was, and is, unknown. You'll never know who he is."

Tricia looked helplessly about her, shoulders sagging.

"If you want a family, Tricia," Randall said gently, "appreciate Jim and Barbara. They're your parents. And," his voice hesitated as he reached to move a wayward strand of blond hair that had fallen out of place. "And someday you'll fall in love, marry, and have children of your own. A family of your own."

"Fall in love," Tricia echoed in a whisper, realizing that one cherished dream was being taken away from her and another one offered. She couldn't let them both slip from her grasp. She must find some way to make Randall understand. "Not some day, Randall. Now. It's already happened. I've fallen in love with you."

"Could it be? Could I be the one?" he asked.

With shining eyes, Tricia nodded.

"Then marry me, Tricia. I love you. I have since the first moment I saw you. Marry me. I swear I'll make you happy."

"But you said you were too busy for me."

"I did?"

"Yes. At the hospital, before I left with Harry. You said you were too darned busy."

"And you thought I was just dismissing our relationship?" he asked, incredulous.

"What was I supposed to think?"

"Oh, Tricia. What a mess we keep making of our lives."

"What can we do?"

"To start, I'm hiring another doctor to share my duties at the office. Then I won't be so busy. There won't be so many interruptions in our lives together. I've already set up interviews with several people who are interested, doctors who would be an asset to this community. I don't know why I didn't think of it sooner."

Tricia smiled. "You'd do that for me?"

"For myself. I love you, Tricia. I can't imagine living without you any longer. I won't allow anything to come between us again."

"Oh, Randall, I love you too."

"Love is a good reason to get married," he said, suddenly playful, as he wrapped his arms tightly around her as if he never intended to let her go again. He looked down into her face. "But isn't there another reason you should marry me?"

"Because of . . . " She looked at him quizzically. "What, Randall?"

"Nicholas needs children to play with."

Tricia smiled. "Our children?"

"Yes," he answered. "All girls. Daughters to contend with Matthew, Mark, Micah, and Marty. Four girls, and every one of them as beautiful as you are."

Chapter Twelve

Randall emerged from the delivery room, still wearing the green smock, pants, and cap his profession required. He carried a small sleeping bundle wrapped in a pink blanket in his arms and faced the nervous group that had gathered in the waiting room during the night. As if one, Harry, Emily and Bradley and their five boys, and Jim and Barbara rose and approached him, tentatively reaching out to touch the precious bundle he carried. "It's a girl," he said softly as if afraid a loud noise might break the spell of enchantment he'd lived under for almost two years.

"How's Tricia?" Barbara asked.

"She's fine. She's wonderful," he answered without taking his eyes from his daughter. "Vince is still in with her, but she'll be out soon and ready for everyone to tell her how beautiful our baby is."

181

Reluctantly Randall extended the sleeping child to Matthew. "Tricia says you're to hold the baby first because today is your birthday."

Matthew, with a look of awe on his face, carefully took the sleeping form, aware of the privilege being awarded him. His boyish features softened as he examined the round pink face and wisps of blond hair. "I guess this means we aren't going fishing today, huh, Uncle Randall?" he asked without disappointment.

"No fishing today," Randall agreed, his own voice echoing the awestruck tone of his nephew. "We have to think of a name for your cousin."

"Hey, I have a birthday next month," Micah interrupted, looking over Randall's shoulder at Matthew and the baby. "But I want a boy cousin for my birthday, not another girl."

Everyone laughed at Micah's request, ending the churchlike hush. Everyone began chattering at once, hugging each other and maneuvering for a better view of the new arrival.

"There will be more," Randall promised, running his hand affectionately through Micah's hair, "but not in time for your birthday."

A white-clad nurse appeared in the doorway. "Dr. Land, Dr. Johnson said to tell you we're ready to move your wife to her room now."

Randall took the baby from Matthew, who seemed reluctant to give her up.

The nurse smiled. "As soon as we have Mrs. Land settled, you can all take turns coming in to visit her and the baby."

As soon as Randall's back disappeared through the

doorway, Harry began organizing the visitation schedule. ''Jim and Barbara will go in first because they're the grandparents,'' he announced with an air of much importance in his voice. ''Next will be Emily, Bradley, and the boys.''

''What about you?'' Emily asked, wondering about his sudden calm after nine months of nervous anticipation, during which he'd walked Tricia around the park each morning because Randall had said it would be good for her, and carved a beautiful wooden cradle fit for the child of royalty.

''I'll go in last,'' he stated, getting comfortable in a chair. ''It's only fair, because I'll be the one who gets to see her most often. My house is right in their backyard, you know,'' he explained, as if everyone was not already aware of that fact.

Back in her room, Tricia held her firstborn child as Randall sat beside her and looked on lovingly. ''You were wonderful, Tricia,'' he whispered approvingly, reaching out to touch both mother and child. ''So beautiful and brave.''

The door burst open and Vince entered with bottles of Champagne and three glasses. ''It's time to celebrate,'' he announced. ''I thought the day I was best man at your wedding was the happiest day of my life,'' he said, popping the cork noisily from the bottle. ''But I was wrong.''

He poured from the bottle—full glasses for he and Randall, who had together delivered the beautiful baby—but only a little of the nonalcoholic variety for Tricia, who would be nursing the infant.

"A toast?" he asked, handing her the glass.

Tricia thought. "To the future," she said. "To good friends, a wonderful husband, and many, many more days like today."